"Us?"

"Don't pretend you don't know what I'm talking about," he said. "I thought I had made it abundantly clear this morning where I want our relationship to go. You're the only thing holding up progress."

Carol flushed, memory curving her lips with a gentle smile. There was no doubt that Zach Taylor held the key to the passionate part of her personality. She became liquid in his hands, and she loved touching him and being touched by him.

Zach's husky voice was seductive, rolling across the telephone. "Are you remembering? Thinking about what almost happened?"

Dear Reader,

Welcome to Silhouette. Experience the magic of the wonderful world where two people fall in love. Meet heroines who will make you cheer for their happiness, and heroes (be they the boy next door or a handsome, mysterious stranger) who will win your heart. Silhouette Romances reflect the magic of love—sweeping you away with books that will make you laugh and cry, heartwarming, poignant stories that will move you time and time again.

In the next few months, we're publishing romances by many of your all-time favorites, such as Diana Palmer, Brittany Young, Emilie Richards and Arlene James. Your response to these authors and other authors of Silhouette Romances has served as a touchstone for us, and we're pleased to bring you more books with Silhouette's distinctive medley of charm, wit and—above all—*romance*.

I hope you enjoy this book and the many stories to come. Experience the magic!

Sincerely,

Tara Hughes
Senior Editor
Silhouette Books

OLIVIA FERRELL
Cajun Man

Published by Silhouette Books New York

America's Publisher of Contemporary Romance

SILHOUETTE BOOKS
300 E. 42nd St., New York, N.Y. 10017

OLIVIA FERRELL

was born and raised in Missouri. Having worked in various fields, ranging from modeling to advertising to radio broadcasting, she tried her hand at writing in 1981. When not reading or writing romances, Olivia divides her time between her three children and her husband, Tom, who is a successful artist.

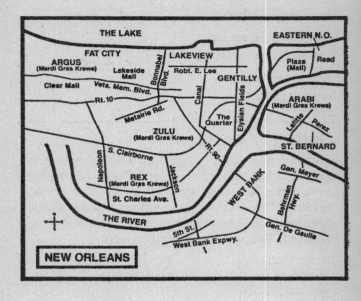

Chapter One

Zachary Taylor strolled into the small restaurant in the New Orleans French Quarter a few minutes after noon. His slow stride and leisurely bearing were the perfect cover for the intensely curious and questioning mind behind his black eyes.

It had been several years since Zach had seen John DuBois. Though surprised by his call, Zach was looking forward to a reunion with his college friend over lunch.

John was already seated at a table nursing a drink. When he saw Zach approaching, John rose and waited expectantly. Zach could see that John had changed little over the years between his college graduation and now. A little extra weight, a little thinning of the hair, a more conservative style of suit. More startling, however, were the deep lines across his forehead and about his mouth. John DuBois was the picture of a harried man.

"Zach, it's good to see you."

"And you, John." With an indolent air, Zach seated himself across the table from John, noting with passing interest the stares of two women seated nearby. He granted them a lazy smile before turning his concentration on John DuBois.

John took a sip of his drink. "Do you want something...?"

"No, thanks." Zach studied the man seated across from him with veiled curiosity. He seemed nervous, uncertain, but Zach waited until the waiter had departed before opening the conversation again.

"Well, John, tell me about yourself."

Drawing a deep breath, John ran restless fingers through his hair before speaking. "You must think I'm a jerk, calling you out of the blue like that after so long."

"Not at all. We were fairly close at one time. Fraternity brothers. As people do, we drifted apart, but that doesn't mean I won't help you if I can."

"Is it so obvious I'm in trouble?"

"John," Zach said, recognizing the prevarication, "what can I do for you?"

"I called on impulse. I feel a little strange now about asking you." He fidgeted with his glass.

Zach leaned forward, his elbows on the table. "Look, John, whatever it is, it can't be as bad as you're making it out to be. What's wrong? Family, business—what?"

John expelled a long breath of resignation. "Business."

"The electronics firm?" Zach asked, beginning with basic questions, trying to put his friend at ease, to draw him out a little.

"You may not have heard, but my father died a couple of years ago. He left me the family business."

"I heard. You kept the business to run yourself?"

"Yes, but just before he died, Father went into computers. That's the big thing right now, and he was farsighted enough to get into it big ahead of most. But that's the problem. I don't have the flair he did, and I'm in trouble." He took another healthy sip of his drink.

Immediately Zach's mind went into action while outwardly his demeanor remained one of casual interest. "What kind of trouble and how big?"

John seemed to relax a little, as if recognizing he'd found help. "First, tell me what it is exactly that you do. I've heard about you often over the past few years. You've built quite a reputation in New Orleans as well as outside Louisiana."

Natives of the city, both men spoke with a soft drawl, slightly slurring the syllables of the city name so that it sounded like "Naw-luns."

"Then you have a good idea of what I do, John. Basically I'm a consultant. I specialize in advising businesses that are in trouble, either managementwise or financially, and finding a way to salvage them."

John nodded, the tightness in his face relaxing a little. "Good. That's what I wanted to hear, because I have a real challenge for you."

"Go on." Zach was interested.

"The business my father left me was doing well. It had survived the move into a new field. Then Father died. His death was unexpected and sudden, and I was totally unprepared to take the reins." He looked up at Zach with a wry twist to his mouth. "You know what kind of a bookworm I was in college. In fact, we met at the library, didn't we? I spent most of those four years there."

"I know. Your major was...political science, wasn't it, with a minor in history?"

"Yes." John smiled for the first time. "And yours was 'biology.'" When Zach returned the grin, acknowledging John's reference to Zach's campus escapades with the female students, John continued. "There couldn't be a more unlikely candidate for heading up a computer company than me."

Zach shrugged noncommittally. "So, what's the problem?"

"Everything, it seems. Production is fine, but installations are down and we have a warehouse full of equipment I can't push. So, we're going into the red nearly every month, and if it continues, well, I'll have to sell—if I can find a buyer. Otherwise, it's bankruptcy. I don't want to do that, Zach. I can't admit failure. Father would roll over in his grave."

"I see." Zach thought for a long moment, analyzing what John had told him. "Can you pinpoint what the problem is? Is there someone undercutting you?"

"That's about it in a nutshell. CCC, Computer Components Company, is undercutting every bid we make. It almost looks like they've zeroed in on us in particular, taking away every job we bid on. We've tried talking with them, trying to find out what's happening, but we can't get a lead on anything. It just seems that they know everything we're doing." He thrust his long fingers through his hair again, making it stand up in ridiculous spikes. "It's as if we're being deliberately sabotaged."

"Do you have any enemies, someone holding a grudge?"

"No, no one that I can think of. Just professional competition. Look, Zach, we're not a big company, but we have a reputation for doing business honestly, for standing behind our product, for sales and service second to none. But something is happening that's out of our control. And to make it even worse, I can't find out anything. It's the most frustrating situation I've ever found myself in."

"And what would you like me to do?" Zach settled deeper into the plush captain's chair.

"I'd like you to find out why they're doing this. Whether they've got a legitimate complaint or it's a vendetta of some kind, I'd like to sit down and talk it out. If it's strictly business, I'd like to know why they've picked on us. I know it's not the kind of thing you do, and it's a small job, but . . . I would consider it a big favor, Zach, and we'll pay whatever fee you set."

Zach Taylor waved a hand in the air to indicate dismissal of the offer. "Don't worry about that. I'm intrigued. Do you know who owns CCC?"

"No. Apparently it's a tight group. The word is the company's owned by an out-of-town association."

"Hmmm. Well, I'll start on it this afternoon. I have some sources not readily available to outsiders. Maybe they can give us a few clues. Meanwhile, let's order and you can tell me something about what you've been doing the past ten years."

They ordered typical New Orleans cuisine—bisque, a thick soup made with shellfish, strong black coffee and, to top off the meal, wedges of pecan pie.

"Have you ever married, John? Wasn't there a little blonde you used to run around with a lot? Carol was her name, I think."

For the first time John's face relaxed in a smile. "I wasn't the ladies' man you were, Zach. Carol was, is, my sister."

"Oh, that's right. I forgot. She didn't go to Loyola with you?"

"Nope. We're different as day and night. We're twins actually, but you'd never know it to look at us. And our interests are totally opposite. Carol went to Louisiana University—against Dad's wishes—and took a business degree. He was a little chauvinistic about her place in the world, thought she should stay here and concentrate on marrying the right man and producing grandchildren. But Carol had other ideas. She moved out, graduated with honors and never came home again. When Father died, she returned for the funeral but flew out the same afternoon." He shook his head wonderingly. "I don't know much about her. We didn't have time to talk then, things were such a mess. And it was like talking to a stranger, the hour or so we did have together."

"Your mother is dead?"

"Yeah, died when Carol and I were about twelve. A bad time for a girl. My father wasn't understanding about her problems, and she wasn't about to accept his plan for her life. They fought a lot."

Amusement curled Zach's mouth into a smile. "I only met her once, but I remember her as a feisty little girl. I seem to remember curly blond hair, bright blue eyes, an easy smile—though I don't think she was much given to teasing. I think I commented on her height, 'five-foot-two, eyes of blue'—that sort of thing, and she was definitely hostile."

"That's Carol. Prickly as a porcupine and she has the biggest chip on her shoulder you ever saw. From what I saw at the funeral, she hasn't changed much.'' John pushed back his now empty pie plate. ''How about you? Are you married, children?''

Zach refilled his coffee cup from the carafe on the table. ''I tried that. Remember Stacy?'' At John's hesitant nod, Zach continued. ''Red hair, freckles, head-cheerleader type? Well, we made the mistake of marrying. It lasted two years before we finally agreed to disagree and divorced. Fortunately there were no children.''

''What happened?'' John prompted when Zach let the explanation die.

''Oh, general boredom with each other. We grew apart, and there was never really anything substantial there to begin with. It just took us both a couple of years to face the truth. We had both been in love with being in love, forgetting the commitments involved. It was best to end it while we could still be friends.''

''You still see her?''

''Occasionally. She moved away from New Orleans, made a career of her own, which was the best thing she could have done. It's still a painful thing for me to think about. What about you?''

''Never married. Like my books too much for anyone to put up with me. Almost got engaged once, but it didn't work out. It's just as well.''

''And Carol?'' Zach prompted. He remembered her as a quite intriguing girl of twenty and wondered how she had grown up.

''She married, but they divorced. Career conflict, I think she said. Something of that sort. She wasn't willing to discuss it at all, and none of us ever met the guy. Strange girl, Carol. I often think we should have exchanged positions. She was much more stubborn and determined—something Father hated, although he also admired that a little." John toyed nervously with the corner of his napkin as he lost himself in thought for a moment.

"Well, I'd better get on with the business at hand." Zach picked up the tab for the meal, overruling John's protest. "If I have anything for you by the end of the week, I'll give you a call." Fishing into the breast pocket of his jacket, Zach extracted a business card and handed it to John. "Meanwhile, if you have anything to add to what you've told me, don't hesitate to call. My home number is on the back."

Zach turned right as he left the restaurant, deciding to walk back to his office, which was situated near the heart of the business district. From his office, he could look down on Canal Street. One hundred and seventy feet wide, the street boasted New Orleans's largest department stores and best hotels. Farther north, the street changed to a tree-shaded residential avenue that ended in an area called *the Cemeteries*, which held some of the city's oldest and most historic graveyards.

As he walked, Zach drew a deep breath. This was *his* city. It smelled wonderful, the air fragrant with the aroma of food and people and trees. After college he had willingly centered his business interests here because he could not imagine living anywhere else.

At first he had been content with working in corporate headquarters, managing the far-reaching interests of his family. But eventually that had not been enough, and he had branched out on his own, quickly gaining a good reputation as a skilled businessman willing to turn his considerable talents to rescuing companies in trouble.

His family had not been pleased, but after the death of his parents, he had continued to keep a steadying hand on the family interests, as well as running his consulting firm.

It hadn't been easy at first. He'd had to overcome the laziness of his college days. Learning came easily to him, and he had skated through the six years of school with an air of indolent acceptance of his position in society and in the scheme of things in general. He still carried with him an air of self-assurance; he was a man who had carved his own niche and was proud of his successes.

Walking with a long energetic stride, his hands shoved into his trouser pockets, Zach looked over his city. With a reputation for being one of America's most interesting cities, it was nicknamed the City Care Forgot because the citizens were always ready to lay aside their business to have a good time.

Zach would often look out over the city from his office and experience its excitement. The main part of the city was wedged between the mighty Mississippi, which swept past to the south, flowing east in a giant bow, and Lake Pontchartrain to the north. He had lived in the city all his life, and he loved the infectious excitement that built in him whenever he looked at it. Zach drank in the heady atmosphere as his long strides carried him quickly back to his office.

Meanwhile, in another part of the business district, a conversation was taking place by telephone.

The CCC offices, although not as impressive as those of DuBois Electronics, were a flurry of activity.

A woman of about fifty sat outside an office door marked only by a small metal plate with roman-style lettering spelling out "J.C. Martin." She picked up the telephone when it rang.

"J. C. Martin's office, Anita Browne speaking. Oh, yes, J. C. The mail is in and we got the bid on the Collins project. Yes, I thought that would please you." She listened for a moment. "That bid went out this morning. Yes. Are you coming in today? All right, I'll send those out before noon." She listened briefly again. "Yes, we were able to learn quite a bit about Zachary Taylor. It's in the packet I'm sending you. Briefly, he's from an old New Orleans family, the rich son of a rich man. He's controlling the family fortune, heavy into investments, and besides that he's had his own consulting firm for the past five years." Her narration was halted by a comment on the other end of the line. "Personally? Well, he's unmarried, thirty-four years old, a graduate of Loyola University with a degree in business administration. He was married briefly in his twenties, but it ended with a quiet divorce. Apparently he's avoided becoming involved seriously since. He has cut quite a wide path through the eligible women of New Orleans society, though." She shifted the telephone to her other ear. "That's about it, J.C. He's interested in the historical society, likes jazz, lives in the old family home in the Garden District."

Again she listened. "Yes, there are several pictures in the packet I'm sending you, candid newspaper pictures as well as a couple of posed publicity shots. Considering his social prominence, they weren't all that easy to get, let me tell you. Had to contact the historical society with a trumped-up story."

After a few more minutes the conversation ended and Anita Browne sealed the packet that bulged with information about Zach Taylor. She then buzzed for a messenger to deliver it to her employer.

It was late in the afternoon before J. C. was able to get to the packet that had been delivered to her hotel room shortly after noon.

Having ordered coffee from room service, she sat down at the desk and slit open the envelope with long manicured fingernails. Spilling out the contents, she studied the five by seven photos first, settling back in the chair with a coffee cup poised halfway between the saucer and her mouth.

"Well, well, it is the same Zachary Taylor. It truly is a small world," she said quietly to herself, before finally sipping the cooling coffee.

Electric-blue eyes skimmed the glossy photos and the blurry newsprint once again. He was the same. With his dark good looks, his Creole heritage obvious. It was Zachary Taylor looking out at her from the photos. She remembered the assessing and sensual quality of his black eyes. There was a hint of his quick smile—the parenthetical lines that were just beginning about his mouth. And she remembered the crisp dark hair that, in college, he'd worn long and carelessly unruly. Now it was more controlled. There had been a lazy indolence in him then, and she wondered just how much of the play-today-work-tomorrow personality remained in him.

Again she studied the photos spread across the desk before her. Zach's face was angular, the wide forehead tapering into a narrow but determined jaw. Not seen in the pictures was the husky voice she remem-

bered from that brief introduction or the athletic build
of his six-foot frame or the strong hands that had held
her own just a bit too long, sliding away seductively at
the last minute. She remembered thinking he was a
jock, a big man on campus and unworthy of her interest, but he had been compelling all the same, his
charm genuine. She had been impressed, reluctantly
so, but getting an education had been dominant in her
mind at the time.

Though they had never met again, Zach had occasionally come into her thoughts when business brought
her to New Orleans, but she'd never before followed
through on the thought of checking up on him. Now
it had become necessary, if her plan was to work, to
know just who her adversary was.

Slowly J.C. pushed aside the photos and began
reading the clippings her secretary had sent. Before the
pot of coffee was gone, she had finished reading and
her mind was busy putting together a plan in which
Zachary Taylor figured prominently.

By Friday Zach had learned a little about J. C.
Martin. He telephoned John DuBois to report.

"You were right, John. No one is talking about this
J. C. Martin or CCC. It really makes me curious."

"What were you able to learn?"

Zach lifted a sheet of paper from the folder before
him on the desk and read from the typed information
sheet. "Well, as you know, CCC is six years old, for-
merly wholly owned by Gerry Carson. About a year
ago, when Carson died suddenly, this J. C. Martin
took over the reins and went public with some stock to
get an infusion of money, but he retained a majority
of the shares. After taking six months to reorganize,

the company is more solid than ever, and suddenly it's very competitive in all areas of computer components and installation.''

''Well, that's a start, Zach. I remember something about Gerry Carson and CCC before this Martin took over. It was a failing company. Carson spent his younger years living up to the family reputation for fast living. Married a socialite who agreed with his lifestyle. She died unexpectedly about two years ago, and Gerry turned to drinking. The business was something like this one, an old family concern, but he revamped it six years ago. You haven't been able to learn anything more?''

''Not yet, but I'm still digging. With only initials to go on, no previous business record and no leads on where he came from, this Martin is really hard to uncover. It appears, though, that CCC may be part of a conglomerate and it'll be difficult to track down the real head of the company. But we'll get it done. Have you heard anything more from your sources?''

John sighed. ''No, just that we lost another project. A rather lucrative one. It would have put us in the black for this month, just barely, but in nonetheless. Of course, it went to CCC.''

Dejection was evident in John's voice, and Zach's brow creased in a frown. Even in college, John had been a rather passive fellow, more interested in the theory of things than the reality. A man of practicality and learned logic, Zach had not been able to understand the rather cerebral younger man, but they had become friends. The difference in interests as well as in years had not been important when it came to classes they had together.

"We'll find out what's going on, John, and then decide how to handle it. Don't worry."

After he hung up, Zach went back to the file, re-reading everything before taking the next step. It might be necessary to go to Computer Components and beard the lion in his den, but he wanted to learn a little more first.

Chapter Two

Anita Browne spent so much time talking to her absentee employer that she was beginning to think the telephone was a permanent part of her anatomy. It was definitely a strange way to do business, but J. C. Martin rarely came to the office, preferring to remain in her hotel room when in New Orleans. Generally she conducted business by long distance from Baton Rouge or Shreveport or from out of state. Anita didn't understand any of it, but she dutifully read from the ornately printed card now held in her hand.

"The invitation is for a charity function in connection with the Spring Fiesta. The historical society is supporting a charity ball the night before the tours of famous homes in the French Quarter and Garden District are scheduled to begin. I don't know how they got your name. Shall I just send regrets along with a check, as usual?" The Spring Fiesta was an annual event celebrated shortly after Easter, featuring tours of plantations and of homes in the city.

Surprise marked Anita's face at J. C.'s response. "You're going?" She quickly regained her composure. "Of course, I'll respond as you wish. It's a costume ball, J. C. You're to come in antebellum costume, naturally."

After a few more minutes the conversation ended. Anita slid a slate-gray sheet of notepaper into the typewriter and quickly tapped out, "J. C. Martin accepts your kind invitation to the Historical..."

The hotel was brightly lit, and expensive cars of varying description left guests in dazzling costumes of pre-Civil War era at the entrance. The large ballroom was aglitter with decorations, beautiful gowns and jewelry. A string quartet at one end of the room played background music to the growing murmur of conversation. There would be dancing later.

The bar was busy and the buffet table was laden with a variety of delicious food. Guests milled about, groups forming and breaking with a constant rhythm as friends and acquaintances mingled. Zach Taylor, dressed in a replica of his great-great-grandfather's Confederate colonel's uniform, hesitated in the doorway, his dark gaze skimming the guests. He wondered if J. C. Martin was among those who had already arrived.

A blue-eyed gaze flicked across the room and settled on the tall man in the uniform who was hesitating in the doorway. Her features concealed behind a silver and lace mask, the speculation on J.C.'s face was well hidden. She sipped the glass of iced tea held in one hand while balancing a plate of assorted hors d'oeuvres in the other. She could almost smile, reading the thoughts behind the handsome face. Zachary Taylor was wondering if she was here. Soon, she promised him silently. Soon you'll get your wish. We'll meet again, and you'll get the surprise of your life.

The evening progressed quickly. A substantial amount of money was raised to support the restoration of a building the historical society had targeted for preservation, but Zach was no nearer determining whether the elusive J. C. Martin was in attendance. There was such a crowd, and the constant milling kept him from being very effective in separating those whom he already knew from strangers. The masks didn't help at all.

He had, however, noticed a blond woman in a beautifully designed pale blue dress whom he could not readily identify. His curiosity piqued, he began watching for her while continuing to scan the crowd for any unidentified man who could be J. C. Martin. The object of his interest suddenly appeared before him.

"Zachary Taylor?" The low voice caught his attention. Zach looked down into the most incredible blue eyes he'd ever seen. They were large and wide, their near-violet shade intensified by the dark fringe of eyelashes, and the bordering mask.

For a long moment they simply stared at each other, completing their individual assessments. The woman's pale blond hair was drawn up and fastened at the crown, and ringlets fell to her shoulders in a charming bouncing arrangement. With her hair drawn back from her heart-shaped face, the delicacy of her pale skin was more obvious. Her mouth, forming the syllables of his name, was cupid-bow shaped, her porcelain teeth perfect as they were revealed by a small smile. Her nose just missed being up tilted. Her chin was small and rounded. The oval shape of her pink-tinted nails tipped perfectly her long slender fingers and graceful hands, which held a glass of iced tea. Zach completed his quick appraisal of her, noting the eyes held something familiar that he could not place, and watching her smile again in recognition of his perplexity.

"Yes?" he responded, wondering why she had sought him out, though grateful for it.

"I didn't think you would remember me. I'm Carol, John DuBois's sister."

Zach blinked in surprise. "Carol? I didn't know you were in town. John hasn't mentioned it."

"He doesn't know I'm here."

Warily he studied her again. "Why not? He's your brother."

"And he's in trouble. You didn't finish the statement, Zach. I remember you as being a very... thorough... kind of man."

Zach straightened almost imperceptibly, keeping his gaze on her while a brief warning bell rang in the back of his mind. "I don't think you had much of an opportunity to form an opinion of me, considering the brevity of our one and only meeting."

Again she sipped at her drink, her lips curving at the rim of the glass. Standing so close to her he could smell her particular brand of perfume. It was not the light flowery scent many fragile blondes wore. It was heady, musky, woody, and it tantalized his sense of smell as the sight of her teased his sense of sight. Though she exhibited an air of aggressiveness that taunted him, there was a flicker of something in her gaze, in the tilt of her head that suggested a veiled vulnerability.

"You make quite an impact, Zach. I've thought of you frequently over the years and kept track of you. I understand you've developed quite a successful consulting firm."

"Success is relative. I enjoy it."

"You've kept in touch with John over the years?" Again she sipped her drink. He could not help watching the curve of her mouth, and she knew he was caught.

"No. I've done quite a lot of traveling in my business and before that with the concerns of my family's business. But we've been in touch just lately."

"Business?" she queried, watching him carefully.

What is she up to? Zach wondered. There seemed to be a certain wariness in her, which piqued his curiosity.

"Friendship," he responded. "In spite of our differences, we spent many hours talking while pretending to study. I've enjoyed picking up where we left off."

The blue eyes sparkled with humor. "If I know my brother, he filled those hours with theorizing about the political and economic situation of the world and never came up with any concrete answers. He was always good at that."

"John is a very gentle man, Carol. The world needs gentleness." He cocked his head to one side as a question formed in his mind. "What have you been doing since college? John didn't seem to know exactly."

She parried his question. "You've been asking about me?"

He smiled lazily, a teasing quirk to his lips. "The subject arose."

Carol returned his smile, understanding dancing in the wide expanse of her blue eyes. "I've been busy." She set her glass on an available tray and stepped aside as a couple passed. "My degree was in business, and I was fortunate enough to gain a position with a company in Shreveport."

"John said you married."

"Yes, but that lasted only three years. A difference of opinion, you might say."

Zach watched Carol carefully. There was a defensiveness about her that made her words clipped, staccato. "I'm sorry."

Carol shrugged indifferently but she avoided his penetrating gaze. "I understand you suffered the same fate a few years ago."

"I didn't realize that fell under the heading of general information."

"I told you, I've kept up with you over the years."

"Why?"

Carol moved delicately, the low bodice of her dress gaping open momentarily to reveal the faintest shadow of cleavage. She was slender, but she had been when he'd first met her. The shadows at her collarbone made her appear even more delicate and fragile than he remembered. Her pale skin was almost translucent. "A matter of...interest? Your family name rang a bell with me when we first met and I asked John about you. He didn't have much information, of course. He wasn't interested in the backgrounds of his friends, not even out of curiosity. So I did a little digging. When your parents died, it was front-page news, of course, and my interest was pricked again. I've kept tabs on your progress."

"I see." But he really didn't. Of what interest could his professional or personal life have been to the sister of a college acquaintance?

With a small smile, Carol glanced into the milling crowd. "I must go." Then she hesitated. "Tell John 'hello' if you see him again." And with that, Carol DuBois floated away and disappeared into the crowd.

A frown creased Zach's forehead. What was she doing here? He would have to ask John more about his sister. Maybe he had information he wasn't aware of. And Zach made a mental note to do a little investigating on his own into one Carol DuBois.

Deciding that it was futile to try to meet J. C. Martin at such a large event, Zach gave the crowd a final glance before leaving. As he exited the hotel and signaled for his car to be brought around, he caught a glimpse of a dark Mercedes pulling away from the curb with Carol DuBois at the wheel. Watching the red taillights disappear down the street, his curiosity was once again pricked. Whatever Carol was doing now, it was obviously successful.

First thing the next morning, Zach had his people checking into the background of the provocative Ms. DuBois. As soon as he was certain John would be in his office, he telephoned him. After initial cordial greetings, Zach got down to business.

"John, have you heard from Carol?"

"Strange that you should ask. She telephoned yesterday, said she was in town. We're lunching today. Why?"

"I saw her last night at the historical society charity ball. I was very surprised."

"Why?"

"Have you seen her lately?"

"Only at the funeral, like I said."

"But you said you didn't have much time to talk with her. She didn't say what she's doing, who she's working for or in what capacity?"

"No. I assumed it was with Gault Chemicals in Shreveport. She got a job with them after graduation. Why?"

Zach swiveled his chair to look out his window at the city. "I'm not sure, John. Call it gut instinct, or maybe it's just surprise, but I think Carol is up to something. I didn't know her, of course. We met just that once. But she isn't what I expected at all. Give me a call after you see her at lunch and let me know what you think."

"What do you think is wrong, Zach? Do you think she's in some kind of trouble or something?"

A wry smile lifted one corner of his mouth. "No, John, I don't think she's in trouble. But something was on her mind."

"What are you talking about?" The subtleties of human nature were foreign to John.

"I'm not sure, John. Just give me a call after you've seen her. Just to satisfy my curiosity, all right?"

After hanging up, Zach continued to stare out the window. Something nagged at him, something about the woman he'd met last night. He wondered what she looked like out of costume and without that mask. The combination of her fragile looks and that touch of uncertainty veiled by an air of aggressiveness made him wonder about Carol DuBois. She wasn't the same cocky young girl he'd met ten years earlier. And he wondered what had happened in the interim to change her.

Zach spent the rest of the day working at his desk and waiting for John's call. When it came, at about four o'clock, he had just about given up on his sometimes disorganized client friend.

"John, how did it go?" Zach swiveled in his chair to look out over the city.

"Well, I think you were right, Zach. Carol is different. I know we've both changed, grown up, but there's a restlessness...something...I'm not sure what. Of course, we were never very close."

"You said she was a determined young lady. Could that mean ambitious?"

"I think determined is the word. And I think she still is, but something is different. I'm not good at character analysis, even with my own twin. As I said, we're complete opposites. But as we talked, I sensed there were things not being said."

"What did you talk about? What kind of questions did she ask?"

"Oh, general things. About people we knew, the house. She asked about you, for example. I told her you'd mentioned meeting her last night."

Zach winced, wishing he'd told John to say nothing about his call to him that morning. "And?" he prompted.

"She just said that she'd introduced herself and that you were surprised to see her. Nothing much more. Apparently your charisma is slipping. She didn't seem overly impressed."

Zach smiled to himself. "She was impressed enough to do some checking up on me herself, John, and that's what concerns me. I keep thinking there's something here I'm missing, something hovering just out of reach that's important. Anyway, if you talk with her again, don't mention what I'm working on and don't let her know I've asked you to report to me whenever you talk, all right?''

"Okay, but why? What do you think she's involved in?''

"Nothing, really. Just say it's instinct. See you later, John.''

As he hung up the phone, there was a knock on the door and a young man stepped inside. "I've got that report you wanted on Carol DuBois.''

"Good. What have you got?''

The young man slid into a chair before Zach's desk. Rob Blake was one of his researchers, one of the brightest, and Zach knew that if there was anything to learn about Carol, Rob would find it.

"Well, she graduated Louisiana University here in New Orleans the same year her twin graduated from Loyola. She took her degree in business administration, took courses in law, too, I learned. A very bright girl. Graduated with honors, then took her MBA. She went to work for Gault Chemical two weeks after graduation. But I understand that wasn't the only offer she had. Apparently she very carefully scouted several corporations and decided on Gault although it was not the strongest company available to her. The school placement officer said her choice had something to do with Gault's corporate structure.''

"He remembered her after this long a time?'' Zach was puzzled.

"Apparently Carol made an impression. After pulling her file, he described her as ambitious, very analytical in her decision making and very certain of her goals. She picked Gault, he remembered, because of the upward mobility available to her there. Translated, that means they don't have a barrier against women executives.''

Zach's eyebrows jutted upward in question. "Oh? Very career oriented, our girl, Carol.''

Rob pointed a finger at Zach. "Right on. I checked with the people at Gault. They weren't very willing to talk, but I learned Carol went to work there, and before very long she was moving up the corporate ladder. According to her employment record, she continued her schooling, taking classes in investments and in law, which the company paid for, since they were job related.''

"You're talking about all this in the past tense,'' Zach said, his head supported on his hand, his elbow resting on the arm of his chair, one leg crossed over the other.

Rob's brown eyes met Zach's intense gaze. "It is. About two years ago Carol resigned her position with Gault. There was no explanation. She just quit cold. They weren't too happy, but there was little they could do. From that point on, there's nothing.''

Zach stared at Rob. "Nothing? What do you mean 'nothing'?'' He came forward in his chair, his elbows resting on his desk as he speared Rob with a look.

"Just what I said. It's as if Carol DuBois dropped off the earth.''

"She was married. What was her married name?''

"I haven't been able to find anything on that. She wasn't married in Shreveport or the county. I'm not even certain of the date of marriage. She always used the name DuBois at Gault.''

Zach relaxed in his chair, leaning back and lacing his fingers behind his head to stretch his shoulders. "I see. Well, keep digging."

"Why is this so important? I thought you were working for her brother?"

"I am, but I keep thinking there's something about Carol that doesn't click. Call it basic curiosity, especially in light of what you've learned—or haven't been able to learn. It sounds very much like our little Carol is hiding something. I just wonder what it is."

"Could be something to do with the marriage. You said John thought the divorce was connected to a career conflict. It might be more. Maybe he was a wife beater. You never know."

"That might account for the determination edged with a kind of... *Uncertainty* isn't the word I want, but there was definitely something...."

"Sounds intriguing. Well, I'll keep digging."

After Rob left, Zach sat in his chair for a long time, thinking over what he'd learned from Rob and what he'd perceived in Carol, plus John's opinions. He could find nothing more concrete to add to his suspicions and finally gave up for the day.

Driving to the family home in the Garden District, Zach was still thinking of Carol. Later that evening he picked up the phone and dialed the number of the hotel she had told John was her temporary residence. He was put through immediately to her room.

"Hello."

"Carol, this is Zach Taylor."

"Zach, how pleasant to hear from you. I enjoyed talking with you last night."

Accepting her tone of polite small talk, Zach didn't mention that their conversation had been more purposeful than pleasant. "I enjoyed it, too, and I'd like to see you again. Would you be free for dinner tomorrow evening?"

"How nice. Yes, I'd like that. About seven?"

"Fine. I'll pick you up. That was room 217, wasn't it?"

"I'll be looking forward to seeing you again, Zach."

The connection was broken before he could respond. He sat looking at the receiver, and speculation narrowed his dark eyes. Well, step one in the dissecting of Carol DuBois, he told himself.

By seven o'clock the following evening Zach was looking forward with great anticipation to spending an evening with John's sister. He arrived at the hotel exactly on time and rode the elevator to the second floor. His brief knock was quickly answered.

Carol swung the door open and smiled up at him. In spite of herself, she was caught by his dark handsome looks. He was dressed in a black suit that complemented his dark complexion and intensified his black eyes. He was a devilishly good-looking man, she admitted, and when he greeted her, his husky voice strummed her senses. She would have to be very careful with Zachary Taylor. He was an intelligent, astute man, and his aroused curiosity would keep him digging into her background until he learned everything he could. It didn't concern her that eventually he would learn the truth. It only mattered that she make her point before he accomplished that.

Zach's dark gaze swept over her, and Carol was glad she had taken great care with her appearance. Her blond hair was worn straight and long, falling from a side part. She generally held back the right side with a clip, but tonight she'd let it hang free to partially obscure her profile.

The dress she wore was a medium blue that magically deepened the color of her eyes. One shoulder was bare, the close-fitting sleeveless bodice held up by a narrow strap over the other. The skirt fell from a beltless narrow waist to swish about her knees. Carol had purposefully kept her makeup light. A faint blush colored her pale complexion, with only light blue eye shadow to enhance her eye color. Her pale lashes were darkened with mascara, which emphasized the wide innocent look of her eyes.

"Zach, would you like a drink before we leave?"

"Nothing for me, thanks."

"Then I'm ready to go." Carol picked up a small bag and a light shawl.

They rode down silently in the elevator. She could sense the wariness in Zach, and her nerves tightened in recognition of the dangerous game she played. But everything was choreographed perfectly. She'd even worn the same perfume, having noted his reaction to it the evening of the dance. Now if only Zach would cooperate.

Finally Carol spoke, the silence having become uncomfortable. "It seems strange, our going out like this."

A smile curved his lips. Her senses quivered in reaction to his dark masculinity. The woodsy fragrance of his cologne came to her in the confined space, teasing her senses even more. She pushed back a twinge of guilt. It was all for a good purpose, she told herself. Something that had to be done, in spite of the bad taste it left.

"Does it? If you'd given me half a chance that day we first met, we might have gone out then."

Carol tilted a glance up at him. "In college? I thought you looked down on me as a friend's bratty younger sister."

"But you're not younger, and hardly 'bratty.' I thought John said you were fraternal twins."

"We are, but I always looked his junior. Of course, now that's not such a bad thing."

"You're thirty-two but look about twenty-five. Most women would welcome that."

"Sure, but on occasion it's been a problem. You don't warrant much respect when you look like a high school cheerleader. You have to prove yourself constantly."

His smile lightened the intensity of his dark eyes. "I can see that." He flicked the length of hair that brushed her shoulders. "Is that the reason for a more sophisticated style? When we first met, your hair was short and curly."

"Partly, though growing older made that change natural."

They arrived at the lobby. Inwardly she was pleased at the looks they received. Her fragile paleness contrasted with Zach's swarthy handsomeness made heads turn. Unaccustomed pride brought a smile to her lips. Normally it wasn't important how she looked. She habitually dressed to please herself or to fit an occasion. But tonight, she admitted, anticipation of Zach's pleasure had been foremost in her mind.

Zach's car was a classic Corvette that had been restored—at considerable cost she guessed. Carol's gaze moved over its low rounded design with interest. "I'm surprised, Zach. I imagined your car would be the latest model."

After helping her inside, Zach slid into the driver's seat. The interior was black leather, matching the shiny black exterior. The dash was inlaid wood with chrome knobs and had various gauges that she didn't understand.

"I bought this at an auction. It was in bad shape, but I found a guy who specializes in this kind of restoration. I prefer it to newer models."

"I like it," Carol stated. Her own vehicle fit an image and she traded yearly.

"You sound surprised that you do."

"I am. I prefer modern things, but I understand your interests lean toward the historical. Your home is in the Garden District, isn't it?" At his nod she continued. "Is it restored?"

"Partially. I like the historical values, keeping to our roots, if you will. But I don't care for the clutter and dark woods and other materials often associated with the house's period. I've preserved the furniture, but lightened the fabrics and decor. I'll show it to you if you're going to be in New Orleans long enough."

"I'll be here awhile."

"Business bring you home?"

"In a way. But let's not discuss those things. Let's just enjoy the evening. It's a beautiful spring night, and I'm sure you've chosen a perfect place to eat." She slanted a provocative glance upward. "I understand you're a bachelor who's very much in demand in this city of fun and games."

He smiled. "I'm not sure what that means."

"Just that you've quite a reputation with the ladies and haven't been caught yet, at least, not since your brief marriage."

"How did you learn about that?" Passing car lights illuminated his profile as she studied it.

"Friends. A man with your money and interests can't escape the gossip mill, and there are a lot of people willing to speculate on your social life. At least as many as are willing to discuss your business ventures."

"For someone who's been in town only briefly, you've been rather busy investigating me and your brother. From what John said, I gathered you haven't been close since college."

Carol glanced out the window as Zach drove into the Vieux Carré, the French Quarter, which was the oldest and most famous section of the city. The balconies decorated with iron grillwork shadowed people strolling beneath. She could look down passageways into colorful courtyards, which were a feature of the Quarter. During the day, their fountains, flowers and leafy banana trees provided relief from the hot New Orleans sun.

"No, I haven't been back since then."

"Why not?"

His husky voice broke the stillness and disturbed her senses in a way she did not want to recognize.

"There was nothing here for me, Zach. Nothing at all."

She could feel his gaze upon her, but she shrugged it off. There had been nothing for her in New Orleans, and Zachary Taylor wouldn't understand that.

He'd inherited his family business and made a success of it. He would not be able to understand her frustration at being denied that privilege.

Chapter Three

Without further conversation they arrived at the restaurant. It was small, intimate, charming, and Carol like it immediately, although she sensed its dangerous tantalization of her already heightened awareness of Zach.

In short time they were served a before-dinner wine and had looked over the menu. They chose pampano fish with a shellfish sauce. After the waiter departed, Carol waited with unaccustomed apprehension for Zach to open the conversation. She knew she was courting danger to even agree to have dinner with him. Being with him had awakened old dreams. Zach distracted her from her plans, made her question her reasoning.

"Tell me about your business, Zach." Carol forced her mind away from her problems and sought to draw him out a little.

"I imagine you know about that already, if you know anything about me at all. The consulting business is a pet project of mine, something I'd thought about since college."

"Then why didn't you go directly into it?" she asked, sipping her wine. It was no longer a matter of business that she questioned him. It was for her own interest.

"I'm an old child and my father's health was already deteriorating when I finished college, so I went into the family business, as expected."

"Was that what you wanted to do?"

"I didn't think so at the time, but it was good experience. It's inevitable that when you first graduate you think you have the world by the tail. It was fortunate that I had that time to discover it's often quite the opposite. I traded the false security that a degree gives you for the more solid confidence I gained after some practical experience."

A smile curled Carol's lips but didn't reach her eyes. "Yes, that is valuable."

His dark gaze studied her. "Voice of experience?"

"Yes, I'm afraid I fell into that trap."

"I understand you went to work for Gault Chemicals. What was your position?"

"Originally I was an executive assistant. Something not much higher than a secretary in their scheme of things. But then I worked my way up, and things were better. At least I had a good position when the truth hit that experience is a necessary companion to education."

"And now what are you going to do?"

Suspicion sharpened her blue gaze. "John is a fountain of information, isn't he?"

Zach chose to be direct. "John is in a lot of trouble. Are you here to help him out?"

A cold hand gripped her stomach. Zachary Taylor was not a fencer. He was a man who got directly to the point. "I don't think that would be a wise move. Like most men, John has a fragile ego and a certain amount of pride. He wouldn't want me to interfere in his business."

"Even though that business was established by your father and is on the verge of bankruptcy?"

She forced herself to meet his gaze directly. "Is it? John hasn't said much about that, but then, of course, he wouldn't. You see, there were a few words of anger exchanged when father left the business entirely to John."

Zach pushed back his chair as he studied her set face. His jacket fell open to reveal the pristine whiteness of his shirt stretched across the hard contours of his chest. "I didn't realize that. What happened?"

Carol considered her words carefully, wondering just how much to tell Zach. "As twins, John and I are supposedly equal in every way. But there are big differences in our personalities. John is the bookish one, more at home in research than in heading up a corporation, no matter how small that corporation. I was always more logical, more aggressive." She drew a deep breath and felt his gaze touching her. "Unfortunately my father held to the view that the older *son* should inherit the family business, regardless of qualifications. Nothing I said made the least difference, and John, being John, did as father willed without question." Carol turned her wineglass about between her fingers.

"And?" Zach prompted when it seemed Carol would not continue.

"And I was out on the street, so to speak. I finished my degree and went out on my own to prove my worth to my father. Unfortunately he died and the will stood."

"Do you really resent that so much?"

Her gaze sharpened, and she was not careful to disguise the intensity of it. "Yes, I resent it. It would have been so much better for me to have been put in control of the company or at least to have been named codirector. But nothing I said made any difference. Father laid down the law—I would marry, bear children and mind my own business. I'm surprised he didn't arrange a marriage for me while I was still in the cradle. He indulged me only so far as to pay for four years of college. The rest I accomplished on my own."

Again he studied her for long moments. "I didn't realize there had been that much friction. John didn't go into it."

"John probably doesn't know the whole story. Most of the conversations between my father and me were conducted in private, though not very quietly. We were shouters, both of us, and emotion ran high. John must have had some idea of the conflict, but it didn't change his determination to carry out my father's will, though, you'll notice. John's got a stubborn streak in spite of his mild demeanor."

"You never told him about your wishes?"

"Zach, John and I were never close. Besides, how could I tell him he was unqualified and put myself forward that way? It had to be proven, to both of them."

"Do you feel you've accomplished that?"

"Not exactly." Again her fingers toyed with the glass, the only outward sign of the nervousness inside her. Somehow this evening wasn't taking the direction she'd planned. She had intended to appear aloof, sophisticated, hard, but here she was, acting like a spoiled, disappointed child. She was giving in to a desire to confide in someone—someone who was objective. But Zach wasn't exactly that. He was in alliance with John to save the company, and she was on the opposite side. The knowledge made her feel a little lonely, and she didn't like it.

"Tell me, Zach, if you had a sister, one who was as qualified to oversee the family investments and sit on the board of the family corporation, would you have allowed her the opportunity to use her mind and talents while you took up your own interests? Would you have been strong enough to do that?"

"I can't really say since that didn't happen to me. Saying, yes I could do that without a qualm, wouldn't prove anything. The situation will never arise and my opinion on it counts for nothing. What you're asking is, did you do the right thing in leaving New Orleans and striking out on your own? And you're the only person who can answer that, aren't you?"

Carol sat, quietly thinking over his statement. "You're a very astute man, Zach. I can see why John turned to you. But, theorizing is John's forte. Let's change the subject. Tell me about you, about yourself. I never had the opportunity to learn anything about you when we first met."

Zach followed her lead. "I think you know most of it already."

"Then tell me about your family. The Taylors are an old New Orleans institution."

He leaned back in his chair again. "Well, my family has been in New Orleans for about five generations. My father's family were among the original Acadians who moved from Nova Scotia to Louisiana in the mid-1700s. On my mother's side, we're Creole, descendants of French settlers in this area. The name, as you may know, comes from the Spanish word *criollo*, meaning *native of the place*, which our family fits perfectly. We've been here a long time. French was the first language in our home, along with the perverted Cajun dialect."

"A Cajun man." Carol smiled, relaxing for the first time that evening.

"A true son of Louisiana," he confirmed.

"Old name, old money. You're a lucky man."

"Your resentment is showing again, Carol." He softened the words with a teasing grin. "Background really means nothing. It's what you do with what you are."

"A beautiful statement, especially coming from someone speaking around the silver spoon in his mouth."

"Your family was not exactly destitute," he fired back.

"No," she admitted, "but certainly not in the class of the Taylors. There was hope for a while—father thought I'd marry money and John would make DuBois Electronics a truly great corporation—but that's gone now."

"You're reverting to old conversations, Carol. Let's let that drop and just talk about us."

Resolutely Carol cleared her thoughts. "All right."

"John said you'd been married. No children?"

"No. And none for you?"

"No."

The conversation lagged. It seemed there was nothing more to say. With unaccustomed nervousness, Carol toyed with her silverware, gratefully acknowledging the approach of their waiter with their meal.

They ate almost silently, commenting only on the fine quality of the food.

"I'd almost forgotten how wonderful everything tastes here in New Orleans."

"It's as good in Shreveport, isn't it?"

"It's not the same. This is home. I guess I'm just realizing what that means."

Zach considered the revealing statement a moment. "You're a strange woman, Carol. Not at all what I expected."

Blue eyes rose to meet his gaze, and for the first time there was a hint of real uncertainty. "Disappointed?"

"No, intrigued possibly or just curious."

"Curious?"

"I'm wondering what makes you seem so on edge. You haven't really relaxed since we left the hotel. Why?"

She forced her gaze to remain direct. "You're a very...disturbing man, Zach Taylor. I'm sure mine is not the first feminine heart to flutter in your presence."

He laughed lightly. "I'm not so certain about that, but I don't think that's the case with you. Is something wrong? Something more than the problem with DuBois Electronics?"

"It would have to be, wouldn't it, since I'm not connected to the business?"

"Would you like to be involved?"

"You've asked that question before, but in a different way. The answer is the same. There is no choice. Unless the business fails or someone buys it, there is no way I can become involved in any significant way."

"If John himself asked you, would that make a difference? It's his prerogative, isn't it?"

"You may be his friend, but you don't know him well. I told you, there's a streak of bulldog loyalty in him that won't allow him to change. It was Father's decision that I be excluded, and John will stick to that."

"Even if it's a matter of the life or death of the business?"

"You'd have to ask John about that."

"But you would entertain the thought," he persisted.

Carol set down her fork. "Zach, you know nothing about my qualifications, my abilities. Why are you so dogged in pursuing this train of thought?"

"You have a master's degree in business and finance, with a backup of corporate law. Your work record with Gault was impeccable, until you chose to leave. But I don't know what you've done in the interim. No one seems to know. Would you care to enlighten me?"

"Let's just say I've taken some time to evaluate my priorities, come to terms with what I want from life."

"And have you?"

"I'm not certain. Only time will tell."

The conversation over after-dinner coffee and pralines was in a somewhat lighter tone, centering around the city of New Orleans and how it had changed since

Carol had left. Very soon they left the restaurant and were back in Zach's car.

"Would you like to take a drive somewhere, see the sights?"

"No, I think I'd better return to the hotel." She glanced at him as he drove from the French Quarter. "I think the evening has not been exactly what you planned, and I'm sorry. It's very unusual for me to be in a situation that's more personal than business oriented. I'm afraid I'm not good at small talk and flirting."

"First dates are often not very comfortable. But I think we did all right. Will you go out with me again?"

She studied his profile, watching the street lights illuminate the strong, dark features of his face. He was a handsome man. An intelligent man. A man who studied and evaluated people and circumstances. The kind of man she'd once looked for, who tugged dangerously at her senses. But it would not be wise to continue this budding relationship. Not wise at all. But her heart was not in agreement with her analysis.

"I'd like that. I promise to attempt to regain some of my lost finesse. Somewhere along the way I seem to have shed some of the Southern belle femininity so important to the Southern gentlemen."

His smile was gentle. "I think I like you better as you are, but not quite so tense. We'll work on that."

They arrived at the hotel, and when he'd parked and indicated he would escort her upstairs, Carol rested a hand on his sleeve to halt his exit from the car. "If you're seeing me out of respect for John, please don't bother. I don't want that."

Zach relaxed in the seat, half turned toward her. In the close confines of the car she was once again arrested by the potency of his maleness, her senses alive and tingling with that awareness. "Carol, we don't know each other well. I hope to change that. But I want to make one thing clear. My business relationships are quite separate from my personal ones. My work with John has nothing to do with my wanting to see you again. If it did, I would change the situation in some way. I want time to get to know you better, to investigate some feelings I have."

For a long moment Carol studied him, attempting to read behind the words, judge the honesty. She was wary of what she sensed happening between them. Emotions were becoming far too complicated much too quickly. If she had paid attention to her logical mind, she would have realized she could not keep herself aloof from this man.

"I'm not sure that's wise. As long as you're working for my brother in even the least capacity, it would be best if we didn't see each other."

"I'm sorry. At this point I can't withdraw from that commitment. John has asked for my help, and I've said I would do what I could. Hopefully, it won't be long until we know what's happening and get the company back on its feet again. I'd like to know that you'll be here when that happens, if you can't see your way clear to continue seeing me before then."

"Then we're at odds, because my business won't keep me here much longer." Carol turned, and her hand was on the handle when Zach's long fingers touched her chin to draw her head back around.

"I don't want to leave it like this."

She watched as he moved closer, his head bending. He was going to kiss her, and she couldn't force her body to respond to a mental command to stop him.

When his lips touched her lips, her traitorous senses opened them to accept his kiss and respond to it. He shifted on the seat, his hand at her shoulder, turning her body to meet his. As his mouth moved on hers, she was conscious only of the excitement racing through her body.

Her fingertips rested on his lean cheek, her senses fully aware of the warmth of his body, the firmness of his lips, the faint scent of his cologne. When his lips lifted from hers, she was aware only of a certain emptiness inside. His dark eyes studied the hesitancy quivering upon her moist lips and traced the delicate features of her face. Something trembled inside her, something that had been dormant for a long time. It was pushing into her and through her. It wasn't something she wanted, but it was a driving force newly awakened that could not be denied.

With his gaze holding hers, he moved away from her and opened the car door. Carol felt as if he'd physically touched her, and she strove to shake off the feeling as he rounded the car to open her door.

With his hand pressing warmly into the small of her back, Carol walked beside Zach into the hotel. Silently they waited for the elevator and rode up in it. At her door she surrendered her key and he unlocked the door and she stepped inside. Zach remained in the open doorway, and Carol turned to face him with an uncertainty that warred with the confidence she demanded of herself.

"I won't ask to come in, though I'd like to. You may be right. We may need more time. But I would like to see you again, Carol. I'll call you in a few days." And with that, he dropped a light kiss across her lips and left her standing there.

Slowly Carol closed the door, shutting out the sight of Zach standing at the elevator. She looked down at her trembling fingers resting on the doorknob. This was an unexpected twist in her plan, a complication she didn't welcome but that could not be denied.

Surrendering to her emotional weakness, Carol slipped off her heels and stepped to the window that opened on the city. Without turning on any lights except the small table lamp just inside the door, she pushed back the heavy drape and looked down on the city.

It was ten o'clock but the city was still wide awake. The Paris of America, New Orleans was called, because of the gaiety and charm of the French Quarter and the carefree spirit of the city. She didn't have the same deep love for the city Zach exhibited, but it had not cradled and loved her as it had him. She forced resentment to rekindle inside her. She needed that burning fire to destroy the seeds of doubt that her evening with Zach had planted.

It didn't matter. None of it mattered. She was here for a purpose, and when that purpose was achieved, she might stay and she might not. It would depend on the outcome of plans already set in motion.

Liar, she called herself. You're not really telling the truth. The day before she had driven out to the house where she'd grown up. John still lived there, but she hadn't stopped. Instead, she had driven past, twice, and then gone on to sit in her car for an hour in one of the parks for which New Orleans was famous.

For a while she had sat there and remembered her childhood, the conflict that had existed between herself and her parents because she would not fit the mold they'd insisted on. When her mother had died, cold silence had grown up between herself and her father.

It began when she was just twelve or so, she remembered, a difficult enough period, since there was no woman with whom to share her insecurities. There was no closeness between herself and John in spite of her wish for more kinship between them.

Unfortunately John had taken after their thoughtful, bookish mother, and during the last months of her life, often sat at her bedside for hours, talking quietly with her. And Carol had been the one too adventurous for her own good.

She sported a broken left arm after falling out of a tree at age six. A treehouse in the backyard was her pet project at ten; she designed and built it herself out of scrap lumber. She spent many hours there alone, crying out her frustrations when her stubborn personality clashed with her father's.

Later Carol even got a job delivering newspapers to earn her own money. Her independence gained her a tongue lashing and a forced resignation from the job when her father learned of it some three months after she'd begun. She had loved that taste of independence. The sense of accomplishment she got from earning her own spending money was something she had never forgotten.

The biggest conflict arose when it had been assumed she would join John at Loyola. Stubbornly, she had dug in her heels and insisted on Louisiana University. Not necessarily because of the curriculum, but because she could be her own person there. Eighteen and just beginning to realize that as an adult she could make her own choices, she'd clashed with her father head to head. Even when her father threatened to end financial support, Carol had not relented. She would pay her own tuition and books if necessary, she'd shouted defiantly. And in the end her father had been the one to relent.

But on one point he had not—that of the future of DuBois Electronics. When she'd learned John was to head the company, Carol had been dumbstruck. Anger, resentment and a certain knowledge that it was not what John truly wanted boiled within her. But John would accept the burden without stating his own feelings. Of that she was certain. And she had momentarily accepted the decree.

It was only later that the real battles had begun, and they ended only upon her father's death. She'd taken law courses to investigate personally the possibilities of breaking the will. She'd toyed with the idea of approaching John and making a place for herself in DuBois in spite of her father's wishes. Frustration drove her from one idea to another.

But nothing had worked. John was not open to the idea. She'd known that would be the case. Even the most tentative suggestion that he might at some time need help was met with opposition. She doubted John had ever fully realized just how unprepared he was for the challenges of heading a growing business in an unstable economy.

Well, she sighed to herself as she turned from the window, you know now, dear John. And you've called in powerful forces to help you. That Cajun man, Zachary Taylor, was good. Everything she had learned about him before tonight showed that. John couldn't have chosen anyone better to save DuBois. And what she'd seen of Zach tonight only enforced that opinion.

Zach was sensitive, thoughtful, a true Southern gentleman, as well as astute, intelligent, resourceful and deceptively aggressive. In a word, he was dangerous—to her and to her plan.

Idly she stood by the desk, her fingertips tracing the initials pressed into the leather of her briefcase. JCM. It won't be long, she told herself. Another week and the tale will be told. And her sense of rightness as to the decision she'd made wavered yet again.

Chapter Four

Rob, three days have passed. You've learned nothing more about this J. C. Martin or about Carol DuBois?" Zach sat behind his desk, his tie pulled loose and the top button of his pale blue shirt undone. His suit jacket was thrown across the couch, and his shirt sleeves were rolled up. Papers scattered around his desk were evidence of the work that had kept him occupied since the night he'd seen Carol.

"Nothing. I'm sorry. It's as if Carol disappeared when she left Gault. Maybe she was telling the truth. Maybe she just took time off and spent it getting her mind together. From what I can learn, judging by the accounts of some former employees, there was a great deal of conflict in the home before she left for college. She lived in the dorm the entire four years before moving to Shreveport. Before now, the only thing she's ever returned to New Orleans for was her father's funeral. It just may be that she learned of the difficulties her brother was having and decided to make herself available. Making a guess at her character, I'd say her pride would not allow her to approach him directly. Apparently, she said some pretty nasty things before leaving the DuBois household for good.''

Zach sat back in his chair and forced himself to relax. ''Yes, I gathered that from John, as well as from Carol herself. And the strain between them still seems strong. I don't think anything will change quickly. I am wondering, though, if John would talk with her and if she did decide to come in with him, whether it wouldn't make the difference between DuBois coming out of this in good shape or dipping too low to be helped.''

''They're in that much trouble?'' the younger man queried as Zach continued to stare thoughtfully across the room.

Zach's gaze shifted to Rob. ''They are. I've done some deeper investigating. John's financial structure is so shaky that one medium tremor could topple it. He's borrowed from Peter to pay Paul without good financial footing, counting on future projects to pay off. That was even before this current problem with being outbid. And that's almost uncanny. It's as if someone was reading his mind.''

''He personally prepares the bids? No one could be leaking the information?''

''Maybe. There's something eluding me here, and it's driving me crazy. There has to be a simple answer to this. Anyway, you keep digging. If you come up with anything new, let me know. Time is running out. If I don't make some decisions soon on DuBois Electronics, there will no longer be a company.''

"Why are you holding back?"

"Because I hesitate to tell John outright he's not operating by sound business practices, especially when that's already a sensitive subject."

"It's tough to tell a friend he's making mistakes, especially in this situation," Rob ventured.

"Yeah," Zach agreed. "And here sits his sister, who apparently is entirely capable of stepping in and taking the reins and turning the whole thing around. I've learned that Carol was instrumental in edging Gault out of its rut as a small-time chemical company and into more innovative and competitive areas. Gault was reputable and substantial but stagnating. I think that's what she saw in that company. She saw potential and took advantage of it. The part I don't understand is her leaving so abruptly. And why is she here in New Orleans now if it isn't to assist John?"

"Maybe it's time to see her again?" Rob suggested.

"I don't want to pump her for information."

Rob shrugged. "Well, I don't know what to tell you. I'll keep digging." And with a salute he was out the door, leaving Zach alone with his thoughts.

In a familiar pose of thoughtful concentration, Zach turned his chair around to stare out the large window behind him. He didn't like the feel of this whole thing. There were too many of the puzzle pieces missing, too many tangled emotions. Someone was bound to be hurt, and he didn't want it to be Carol.

Carol. He glanced at his watch. It was one o'clock. She might be in her hotel room. He reached for the phone, dialed the hotel and asked for her room number. She answered on the second ring.

"Carol? It's Zach."

"Zach, what can I do for you?"

The crisp businesslike tone was back in her voice. It was evident he had interrupted something. Zach toyed with a pencil on his desk, turning it repeatedly in his fingers from point to eraser and back to point. "You can go out to dinner with me this evening."

Carol's fingers gripped the receiver, turning the knuckles white. She wanted to go, but it would not be the wisest thing to do. In only a week or so this whole thing would be over, and she would be leaving New Orleans.

"I . . . don't think so, Zach. Thank you."

"I never thought you were a coward," he taunted.

"I'm not. It's just that you're too involved with John's problems."

"That has nothing to do with us. We don't have to discuss anything even remotely concerning business. We could have dinner, drive down along the shore of Lake Pontchartrain. Just have a relaxing evening. Something casual."

She hesitated, wanting to believe they could do exactly that. Finally she relented, knowing at the same time it was the wrong thing to do. "All right. Pick me up at . . . six-thirty. I should be finished for the day by then."

"Good. Wear slacks, something comfortable. W find a place to eat when we get hungry."

"That sounds like fun." And surprisingly it really did. Normally she did things according to a rigid schedule. Her fingers relaxed on the telephone receiver and a faint smile curved her lips. "I'll look forward to it."

When she hung up, Carol stood for a long moment, just staring at the receiver. What had she got-

ten herself in for? Then she turned back to the open
folders strewn across her desk and absorbed herself in
work once again.

Zach's knock on the door came at exactly six-thirty.
Carol took one last glance at herself in the gilt-framed
mirror on the hotel wall. The oatmeal-colored linen
slacks skimmed her slim frame perfectly. The cotton
knit sweater had a V-neck that hugged her full breasts
in a clinging and alluring fashion. The small cuff on
the sleeve ended just above her elbows, and the ribbed
hem rested on her hips. The leather sandals on her feet
were thin and strappy and matched the shoulder bag
waiting to be claimed from a chair.

When she swung the door open, Carol's glance immediately took in the faded jeans that hugged Zach's
athletic body. The polo shirt hugged the contours of
his chest, and the short sleeves only emphasized the
corded muscles of his arms. The white knit contrasted starkly with the swarthiness of his creole skin.
Compellingly his dark gaze drew her attention to his
face and the smile that curved his lips.

"You look very nice. I like you out of your working clothes."

Her hand rested on the door handle. "I wasn't in
working clothes the other night. In fact, both times
you've seen me here in New Orleans, I've been out of
my working clothes."

His face seemed to hide something. "I don't think
so, my clever lady. I think you were very much working." He stepped inside, and she looked up questioningly as he closed the door firmly.

"I'm afraid I don't follow you."

"I think you do. It occurs to me that we were both 'working,' because we were both bent on discovering something about each other that was not entirely personal in nature. You're in New Orleans for a reason known only to yourself. I have some thoughts on the subject, but I imagine you would deny them even if I were right. As for myself, I'm working for your brother. A brother you don't think capable of running the family business. And while I may agree with you there, I get the impression you're just waiting around for the ax to fall. I don't particularly care for that."

Sudden anger deepened the intensity of her blue eyes. "Blood should be thicker than water? In this case I don't think that applies. John is out of his element. He's a scholar, a research man, a theory person. In a support position he can't be beat. But that doesn't make him a leader." Her fury gathered momentum. "And just what gives you the right to barge in here and make accusations!"

"Your brother's interests give me that right." Equal anger flashed in Zach's dark eyes. "I've been doing some investigating, and what I've learned is very curious."

A knot of apprehension grew in her stomach, and Carol fought for control. "Just what have you learned, Mr. Taylor?"

Her formality pricked his anger even more. "Why don't you sit down! I think we have some talking to do."

Carol stepped back. "I don't think so. You'd better leave. Whatever your business relationship is with John, it has nothing to do with me." When Zach didn't respond, Carol resorted to threats. "I'll call hotel security if you don't leave this minute."

His hand jerked out and long fingers wrapped about her upper arm to draw her nearer to him. His husky voice rasped against her heightened senses. His dark eyes flashed dangerously.

"Don't push it, Carol. I don't like what I've learned, and I intend to find out exactly what's going on here."

With those words Zach propelled her to the couch. His size made it necessary for her to acquiesce, and Carol sat down reluctantly.

Her expression carefully controlled, Carol sought to equally control the pounding of her heart and her accelerated breathing. Firming her mouth and assuming a more relaxed air than the tumult of her nerves would dictate, she forced herself to wait for Zach to speak.

Zach sat near her, intimidatingly leaning forward to hold her attention. She forced herself to meet his gaze and hold it.

"Since John called me in to determine what was happening to DuBois Electronics, I've had a couple of men doing some investigating. That investigation involved you. And what we learned brought up some interesting questions. At first I told myself it was just coincidence that you decided to return to New Orleans at this particular time. After all, this is your home. Your father died here not too long ago. You've been away a good while. Returning was only natural."

"Not everyone has the homing instincts you do, Zach."

His gaze intensified. "I've learned that. I've also discovered that you haven't been entirely honest with me."

Her back stiffened almost imperceptibly as she waited. "I talked with John at length today," Zach continued.

"Before or after you called me?"

His gaze became questioning. "What difference does it make?"

"None, I suppose. Just an idle question." But it was important to her.

"I talked to him after I called you. I told you there is no connection between being with you and doing my job. Yet, I wonder. You're questioning whether I'm using you. Somehow, I had the feeling that's what you were doing."

"What makes you say that?" Carol queried.

"My informants told me that someone's been doing a little investigating of their own into my affairs. I wonder. Is it you? Or is it this J. C. Martin?"

Carol forced herself to remain calm, though her stomach hurt with tension. "J. C. Martin?"

"Yes. It seems that John's trouble began when a firm called Computer Components Company began a full-scale assault on DuBois Electronics. It seemed like a kind of vendetta. When John couldn't learn what was happening, he called me in."

"I would have thought a small firm like DuBois would be out of your league."

"Friendship is a big word in my vocabulary, Carol. About the same size as family and loyalty and commitment. Can you understand that?"

"Your hostility is showing, Zachary. Why don't you explain your point? You do have one, don't you?"

Carol had finally succeeded in slipping into the aloof shell she'd assumed in her career. It worked well for her, keeping a comfortable distance between everyone and herself. It worked now. She could almost see Zach retreating to rethink his approach.

"The point is that you're in New Orleans at a time when John could best use your help. Yet you haven't offered it. Why?"

"That's it? That's what this is all about?"

"Not entirely, but that's a beginning."

Carol stood. With her arms folded, she began to pace the floor, emotions roiling up inside her uncontrollably as she fought not to reveal them to her enemy. And Zach was her enemy now.

"I offered my services to John once. When our father died, I came to the funeral for that purpose. I was busy, very involved in a project for Gault, but I took two days off for the trip in spite of the fact little love had been lost between us.

"At the time I knew what would happen to the company and I offered my help. But John would have none of it. He was determined to prove he could be everything my father demanded, to follow through on Father's desire to have his *son* inherit. It wouldn't do to have a daughter in charge, one whose name might change and who would bring outside blood into the firm." She marched agitatedly back and forth as she spoke.

"Our father was an old-fashioned man. So out of date that the company nearly foundered before... before I found a way to almost force him into exploring computerization trends just beginning to become obvious. He should have known. He should have foreseen what was happening to the economic profile of this country, but he was so tied up in what's always been that he was blind.''

"Just how did you accomplish it?" Zach asked quietly. She seemed to have forgotten he was even in the room.

"Gault was expanding into the same area. One of our representatives was going to be in New Orleans, and I persuaded him to visit DuBois Electronics. He gave my father a copy of some of the research I had done. I could only hope he would read it. He did and began, finally, to do some looking into the possibilities on his own, or rather, he had John do it. That was good. John could understand the technology involved and he was the perfect person to become involved in that area." She shrugged, her anger abated somewhat. "In any event, they soon began some tentative explorations into computers. I was pleased when I saw that. But then Father died and it was all dumped into John's lap. Nothing worse could have happened."

"What did you do?"

She seemed to come to herself then, and Zach recognized that his advantage was gone. "I stayed with Gault awhile longer, then began to reevaluate my priorities, just like I told you."

"And that's it?"

His implacable expression pricked her anger anew. "What do you want, Zach? If it's a life history, you won't get it. It has nothing to do with either you or John. If that's your reason for being here, get out!" His words had hurt, and she fought the pain inside her. She couldn't afford to let him get to her. Becoming involved in any way with Zach was not part of her plan.

Zach rose from the couch and advanced on her. "That wasn't my reason for being here, but now that I've heard this much, I want to hear the rest."

"Get out, Zach," she repeated, retreating a step. "Get out and don't call me again." Her hand encountered the door of the suite's bedroom. She halted, knowing that if necessary, she could step inside and close the door before he could reach her.

"I don't think so, Carol. There are still some questions I have to ask."

"But I have no answers for you. I'm leaving New Orleans. I would have told you this evening."

He stepped nearer, and she forced herself not to retreat again. "Would you? Or would you have just moved out in the morning without telling anyone where you were going? That's what you did at Gault, isn't it?"

"It's my business, Zach. I don't have to answer to anyone."

"You'd leave John with this trouble? You wouldn't feel the least particle of guilt or remorse? He's drowning, Carol, and you could help. Instead, you're throwing rocks."

Her resolve stiffened. "You're out of line, Zach. You're paid to help John, not analyze my motives. Stick to business."

Again he stepped nearer, and she retreated a reluctant half-step. "Business. That's all you understand, isn't it?" Anger flashed in his eyes again, and his face was tight with tension. His body was taut as his hands rested on his hips. Everything in him was accusing her, and she resented it.

"Is that what happened to your marriage, Carol? Were you too involved with your career to be human?

That's what I heard. You spent twelve-hour days at Gault plus weekends, and your total attention was turned to creating a place for yourself there. Well, you succeeded, didn't you? And you sacrificed your husband upon the altar of success!''

His husky voice rasped out the accusations, and the barbed spear of his words embedded themselves in the tender flesh of her consciousness. Old wounds opened and tears stung her eyes. Angry resentment welled up and flooded over as her hands became clenched fists at her side.

Rationality fled. "You... Get out! Get out! Get out!" She flung the words at him in frustration while stepping back into the bedroom and grabbing the edge of the door to close and lock it behind her. But her efforts were thwarted as he stuck one booted foot in front of the closing door.

The jarring effect made her hands tingle. She turned, intending to lock herself in the bathroom. But before she'd taken two steps, his hand reached out and caught her arm, throwing her off balance against the foot of the bed.

The upper portion of her body rested across the mattress, and before she could react and slip away, Zach hauled her fully up onto the bed and pinned her down with his body.

His warm breath fanned her averted face, and his fingers gripped the upper portions of her arms. The hard contours of his chest held her immobile as his heavy thigh was flung across her own to halt her attempts to buck loose of his hold.

"You're going to talk to me this time, Carol. You're going to answer my questions before we leave this room."

"Get off me, Zach." She lurched against him again in a futile attempt to dislodge his hold on her.

"Stop it. I don't want to hurt you." His breathing calmed, but still he held her, willing her to submit.

"I don't believe anything you say." Her own voice was breathy with exertion as she willed her body to remain still in spite of the instinctive desire to free herself of his hold.

"That doesn't really matter. I'm here to listen, not to talk." His body moved along hers as he gained a better hold on her arms. His hands slid down her arms to her wrists, and he held them at her waist with one hand. The knuckles of his hand bore into the soft pillow of her stomach. With his free hand, he grasped her chin to force her face around to him. "Now, I think we have a few things to clear up."

Carol closed her eyes in submission to his superior strength. What a ridiculous turn of events, she told herself. What an idiot thing to have allowed to happen.

"That's better," Zach said, interpreting the relaxing of her body as acquiescence. "Now, for starters, explain why you left Gault Chemicals."

"I told you," Carol repeated stubbornly. "I had to think some things through."

"All this time? You're not an indecisive woman, Carol. It shouldn't have taken you two years to come to terms with whatever was bothering you. What have you been doing all this time? You can't have just been sitting idle."

Carol spoke carefully and precisely, attempting to divert Zach from his mission. "I made a good salary while at Gault. I could afford to take a break."

"Economics has nothing to do with it. In the short time we've had to discover each other, I've found that you're a woman of restless energy. You can't have taken that time off completely. I can't see you just sitting around vacationing somewhere."

Her eyes partially opened to study the tense features of his face from beneath veiling lashes. "Just because you balance two very busy companies doesn't mean everyone else is as driven."

"I think you're well aware that the family interests are now basically philanthropic and almost totally controlled by a board of directors. My own company occupies the bulk of my time. You're the one proving yourself here, not me."

"Oh?" she mocked. "And to whom am I proving it?"

"To yourself. You've eliminated all the others."

Her face hardened as a block of ice formed in the pit of her stomach. "That's your opinion."

"Disprove it," he challenged. "Tell me how many men you've seriously dated in the past two years. Tell me what ties you've established here or in Shreveport, even. I don't think there are any."

"It's nothing to me what you choose to believe."

"Isn't it?" His face came closer, and she could see the individual lashes darkening his eyes, feel the warm brush of his breath as he spoke.

Momentarily they were suspended in the midst of anger. His dark eyes measured the contours of her face, traced the tumble of her blond hair spread across the satin bed covering. Her senses came alive when he continued his inventory of the individual features of her face, tracing the half-closed eyes, the pink outline of her mouth.

Almost unwillingly it seemed, he relaxed against her, stretching his fingers out to spread them across her abdomen.

When he lowered his head, Carol's breath caught. His lips brushed hers, tentatively at first, then more firmly. His tongue tested the barrier of her teeth before the fingers of his free hand tangled in the cascade of her hair to hold her head more firmly. She couldn't have escaped if she'd wanted to, and at the moment she didn't want to.

The palm of his hand pressed into her stomach, making her more aware of her own desires. Her legs shifted beneath the weight of his thigh, and Zach moved slightly to accommodate her. Bending one knee, Carol turned slightly toward him. Need rather than logic now ruled her senses. A desire to be held pushed aside her anger and instinctive defenses.

Her hands now free, her arms lifted to rest on his shoulders. A low groan rumbled in his chest as Zach hunched over her. His hand found its way beneath the hem of her sweater, and when his fingers encountered the soft flesh of her waist, her muscles tightened. His hard palm slid against her skin, forcing the tension to relax before moving upward to encounter the thin fabric of her bra. She arched against him, blind to everything but the desire clamoring inside her.

Everything was forgotten. She seemed to blossom beneath his touch. Her hands explored his shoulders, finally pulling his shirt free of his trousers and hunting for the warm flesh of his back. His bunching muscles played beneath her sensitized fingers and palms, and she reveled in the freedom to touch him. Having him here in her arms had been a dream long dead, but was now resurrected as reality. And nothing else mattered.

Zach worked a sensual magic on her. His hard body pressed her into the mattress. Her bones became liquid, her flesh burning at his touch. And when he trailed soft warm kisses across her eyes and into the feathers of hair at her temple before returning to her searching mouth, Carol lost all semblance of the cool aloof woman who had met Zach at the door.

When her sweater was pulled off over her head, Carol willingly shed the loose strip of bra and pressed her sensitized breasts into the warm flesh of Zach's bared chest. She had not been aware of when he'd rid himself of his confining shirt, but little penetrated what she was feeling inside.

When his hand slid down her spine past the curve of her back and spread across her narrow hips to press her into him, her blood roared in her ears. She wrapped her fingers in the crisp blackness of his hair and brought his mouth down to her again. Her senses ran riot. This was Zach. This was her Cajun man, and she wanted him as she had wanted no man before.

His hand was at the fastening of her slacks when the shrill ringing of the telephone interrupted them. The fifth ring had begun before either of them was fully aware of the sound. The persistence of the caller was evident when the sixth ring began.

His dark eyes searching her flushed face, Zach reached out automatically and lifted the receiver of the bedside telephone. He answered, his rasping voice almost unrecognizable with unreleased tension.

"Hello?"

"J.C.? What's the matter? Are you ill?"

Carol saw the tension in Zach's face shift from passion to anger as his eyes rested piercingly on her. Something about him alerted her to danger, and she began to inch away from him. He allowed her to go, and she looked for her sweater as he responded to the caller.

"No, nothing is wrong. I think all the questions have just been answered." And with those words, he handed Carol the receiver. "J.C., I think this is for you."

Ice froze in her veins where just a moment before there had been raging fire. Nerveless fingers took the receiver and pressed it to her ear.

Chapter Five

Yes?" Carol's voice was breathy with tension.

"J.C.? What's going on there?" Anita's concerned voice greeted Carol's tentative answer.

"It's nothing, Anita. Nothing at all." And she recognized the painful truth of that statement. There could be nothing now between herself and the angry man standing beside the bed watching her. With her arm pressed across her chest to partially cover her nakedness, Carol turned her back to Zach. "What did you want, Anita?"

"You've had another call from Zach Taylor. He wants to meet you for lunch. You name the time and place. Of course, he doesn't know who you are...."

"I think that little problem has just been taken care of, Anita. I'll handle it myself. Is there anything else?"

"I don't understand...."

"Anita, is there anything else?" The edge was back in Carol's voice as she once again assumed the cool facade that was her stock in trade.

"No, nothing. I just thought you ought to know." The woman was obviously puzzled by her employer's curt attitude.

"Fine then. I'll talk to you in the morning. I'll be coming in to the office. Please hold everything until then." She carefully replaced the receiver and sat looking at it for a long moment.

"So, no wonder no one could turn up a background on J. C. Martin. You're J. C. Martin. Your married name, I presume?"

"That's right. Joan Carol DuBois Martin, chief stockholder of CCC, mysterious nemesis of DuBois Electronics. Are you satisfied? Now will you get out of here?" Finally she turned to face the darkly chiseled features of Zach Taylor's angry face.

"No. I still have some questions."

"Then why don't we just wait until tomorrow."

"I don't think that's wise. I would prefer to clear this up right now."

"Zach, just get out of here. I'll see you tomorrow and answer what questions I can." Suddenly she was just very tired—of everything.

He seemed to consider her request for a moment, his dark gaze intense upon her. "No, this has to be taken care of right now. Get dressed. We're going to see your brother."

"No." Her resolve stiffened. "I won't do that. If you're so intent on telling him who I am, then you go see him alone." With determination she forced herself to turn around and locate her discarded sweater. Finding it, she turned her back again and lifted her arms to slide it over her head. With his gaze still on her, Carol ran slim fingers through her tangled hair, automatically smoothing it into some semblance of order before turning to him again.

Unwillingly her gaze went over the bronzed contours of his body, taking in the rounded shoulders, the hard-ridged stomach, the sinewy arms, and tracing the dark T of hair running across his chest and down across his stomach to disappear beneath the belt of his low-slung jeans. He seemed so compellingly male—the perfect opposite of her fragile femininity. And at the moment she felt very fragile, very vulnerable, her senses alive and singing with the knowledge of how easily he could arouse her long-buried passions. Relentlessly Carol quelled the trembling awareness inside her.

"You're going now." Determination firmed his mouth.

"Why?"

"John deserves to know the truth."

"Why should it matter so much to you?" She forced herself to match his intense gaze.

"It's my job, but more importantly, he's a friend."

"I don't understand that kind of friendship."

His gaze wavered not a whit. "I believe there are a number of things you don't understand, but before this night is over that number will have been considerably reduced."

Zach stood there before her, unconcerned that the evidence of their preliminary lovemaking—the rumpled bed, the discarded clothing—was scattered around them. His hair was tousled, strands of it falling over his forehead. His gaze moved over her, retracing the contours he had explored when they hadn't been covered by her sweater. She felt as if he were actually touching her, and her body reacted immediately.

Carol rose and paced away from him. Standing across the room, she felt more comfortable, but still his gaze followed her every movement. She felt like a specimen under a microscope. "This isn't the way to handle it, Zach."

"You have a better suggestion? Like my giving you time to get a plane out of here and disappear so that your company can continue to badger John and drive him to his knees? That's what you wanted, isn't it? To break him, prove how unsuited he is to run the company? Then you could pick it up for pennies on the dollar and take control, just as you wanted in the beginning." His voice was cold, his countenance implacable. "That was what you were trying to prove, wasn't it? Your superior ability? Prove you were right and everyone else was wrong?"

Faced with his growing anger, Carol accepted his verdict, refusing to attempt an explanation. It would only be thrown back at her. "Yes, that's what I wanted. But I didn't want to ruin John. I wanted to help. But he wouldn't let me. And I won't beg, Zach. I can't do that." She gathered her composure. "Besides, it was already too late. DuBois Electronics was on the skids even before I stepped in." Finally she faced him squarely, almost quailing at the cold anger in his dark eyes. She said what she knew Zach expected to hear. "I researched it carefully. You know how easy that is with the right contacts. I just made a slight contribution to the downward slide in order to make John realize he couldn't run the company alone."

"You selfish, self-centered... How could you do that to your own brother!" His hands became fists at his sides, as if he could hardly keep from throttling her.

"It wasn't like that," Carol insisted, her shoulders slumping with the weight of defeat. "You don't understand. You've had everything so easy. You haven't had to prove yourself every step of the way. You couldn't possibly understand...."

"Then make me understand. Tell me the truth."

"I told you the truth! You refuse to believe it." Once again she fought for self-control. "Look, I'll go with you to see John, this evening if you insist. Call him while I get myself together."

"You stay right here. You have a habit of disappearing."

"I'm not going anywhere," she said wearily. "There's no way out of this room except through that door, and you're standing in front of it. I'm just going into the bathroom to wash my face and comb my hair. Surely you can't complain about that."

Zach was picking up the telephone as she stepped into the bathroom and closed the door. She could hear him speaking in a low voice as she leaned wearily against the sink.

Finally she faced herself in the mirror. Her hair was tumbled and tangled, her eyes feverishly bright, her mouth still swollen from Zach's kisses. When she rested trembling fingers against her lips, she was reminded of the firm warmth of his mouth on hers. Tears stung her eyes as she thought of what might have been.

Drawing a deep breath, she forced herself to attend to the task of improving her appearance. Whatever might have been between herself and Zach Taylor was ruined. She had started out to prove her worth to herself and to John and had succeeded only in totally destroying her relationship with the only man she had desired in years.

Still her body tormented her. She couldn't forget the sensations his sensitive fingers had aroused. Zach Taylor could not be relegated to memory as easily as he had been those years before. And with a deep sigh of acceptance of the fact that she'd created an impossible situation between them, Carol opened the door and faced Zach once again.

Zach was waiting, his shirt once more stretching across his athletic body and tucked neatly into his jeans. He'd combed his hair back into its usual control. There was no evidence of their encounter, and that hurt a little. His gaze quickly measured her.

"Ready?"

"No, but I doubt that makes any difference."

"Very little at this point. Come on, we'll take my car."

On the way out of the hotel room Carol picked up her purse. She preceded Zach into the elevator. The ride down to the street level was silent as was the relatively short trip to her brother's office.

Zach pulled up in front of the DuBois Electronics building. When Carol was slow leaving the car, Zach impatiently took her arm and pulled her out.

"No backing out now, Carol. John deserves to know everything."

"Judge and jury, are you?" Carol quipped, straining to hold on to the self-confidence that was usually second nature to her. She would need every bit of her armor this evening. Later tonight she could give in to the growing need to just lie down, close her eyes and cry out her frustration and loneliness.

In just a few minutes they were in John's office. He stood to greet them, his gaze shifting questioningly from one to the other, taking in the tension.

"What's happening here? What's wrong, Zach? You said it was important."

"It is. I think you'd better sit down." As he did, John's gaze continued to flick from one of his guests to the other. "John, I'd like to introduce you to J. C. Martin."

John blinked in surprise. "What? This isn't J. C. Martin. This is my sister."

"True, but what's your sister's full name?"

"Joan Carol," John recited. "Joan Carol Du-Bois."

"And what is her married name?" Zach persisted. Comprehension bloomed. "I don't know...or didn't know, until now." His pale eyes fastened upon her.

"I think J.C. can enlighten us on the subject of her married name, as well as about why she set out to destroy this company." Zach nudged Carol toward one of the chairs in front of John's desk. "Can't you, J.C.?"

Resigned to revealing at least part of the truth, Carol sank into the chair. The only sign of momentary weakness she allowed herself was to give in to the need to rub her temple with the tips of her fingers, willing the headache beginning there to hold off until this ordeal was over.

"I think I am due some explanation, Carol." John's voice was subdued.

"Tell him, J.C." Zach said mockingly.

Shooting Zach an angry look, Carol faced her brother across the wide desk that had been their father's. "John, it isn't exactly as Zach has indicated. I didn't set out to destroy DuBois Electronics."

"Didn't you deliberately buy CCC when the owner died and go public with enough shares to gain sufficient backing to enable you to undercut any bid DuBois Electronics made on any installation project?" Zach demanded.

"Yes," Carol admitted. "I did. But not with the purpose..."

"And didn't you deliberately alter your name to conceal your identity so John couldn't find out who was cutting the ground out from under him?" Zach prompted. "And didn't you come to New Orleans with the express purpose of witnessing the result of your machinations?"

"I've used the name J. C. Martin on investment purchases for years."

"Explain to us what your purpose was, exactly."

Carol appealed to her brother, who sat silently watching what was unfolding before him. "John, I think we can talk this out between us. Zach has done his job. He's unveiled the culprit in this little scenario—quite dramatically, I might add. I believe we can handle this on our own from this point."

Zach interrupted. "My job isn't finished, Carol, until this company is back on its feet."

"But I can do that." Anger prompted her response, and then she realized what she'd said. "I'm sorry, John. I didn't mean this to happen exactly this way."

For the first time John spoke in his own behalf. His usually friendly eyes were cold and his face was set.

White outlined his tense, set mouth. "Then what did you mean to happen? It seems to me you've accomplished exactly what you set out to do."

Realizing Zach was going to remain where he was until the whole thing was finished, Carol began slowly to explain. "What Zach has said is partially true. When I left Gault, I already knew what was happening here. I became aware of it when I returned to New Orleans for Father's funeral. It was only then that I did a little checking and learned the financial condition the company was in. I saw it would only be a matter of time before things became worse." She leaned forward, the fingers of one hand resting on the desk edge. Zach was forgotten in her need to make John understand what she'd done and why.

"John, your strength lies in books, in your ability to research and interpret. Wasn't it you who read the reports Father was given a few years ago on the future of computerization? Wasn't it you who suggested computers was a new direction for the company when it was wavering between advancement and a downward slide? Wasn't it you who took charge of all the research into which attitude to take, whether to be a distributor of preformed units or to go into manufacturing? And didn't Father follow your advice?"

"Yes," her brother admitted reluctantly. "But what's your point?"

"My point is that Father was the driving force behind this company. His aggressiveness pushed ideas through. He put through changes once they were researched. He found new business and courted it. He was farsighted enough to know something had to be done soon. All I did was leave a little clue. The two of you implemented the idea."

"Meaning?" John prompted, his gaze narrowing on his sister.

"Meaning, that as a team you and Father were good, but alone, you're floundering. You need direction. You need someone strong in the same areas as Father was to balance your talents. I wanted to be that person, but you wouldn't recognize me as a possible source of help. You rejected my first suggestions outright. You wouldn't even listen to me, wouldn't give me an opportunity to outline my plans." She sat back in the chair, her gaze still pinned on her brother. "I took the only road open to me. There had to be some way to make you recognize the company's need for someone to take a more aggressive stance, to make DuBois Electronics a recognized entity in the expanding field of computer distribution. I think I accomplished that."

For the first time John let his smoldering anger show. "You certainly did. Zach was right. You set out to destroy this company, to destroy me, out of jealousy and revenge. And you almost succeeded. If Zach hadn't discovered who you are, you would have completed the task. As it is, I can only be grateful to him for coming to my rescue. Now, I think our business is finished. Get out of here. I don't want to see you or hear from you again. And if you try to ruin me again, I'll see that your name is splashed over the front page of every newspaper I can reach."

Carol was stunned. "You mean you're not going to listen to anything I have to say? Not even now?"

"You've said more than enough. You thought you should have this company. But Father's decision still stands. You're out. For good. CCC is your baby, and you'll have to be content with that. Just keep away from me, or I'll ruin you—any way I have to."

Zach remained silent, and Carol flicked him a brief glance before responding to her brother. Drawing about her the shell that had always served her well, Carol reverted to acid words clipped out in a low voice, evidencing iron control. "Well, that's that." Without looking at Zach, she continued. "If you're finished with me, Zach, I'll catch a cab."

Carol stood, and slowly, so did Zach. John remained seated behind his desk, but when Zach would have followed Carol from the room, John detained him.

"Zach, I'd like to speak with you for a moment, if I may."

"Certainly. Carol, wait for me."

Flashing him a look of dismissal, Carol continued on through the reception area, determinedly heading for the outer door. Once on the sidewalk, she began walking briskly, not caring which direction she took.

The streets were getting dark. Carol strode swiftly down the sidewalk, oblivious of everyone and everything. It would have worked, she told herself. It would have worked if Zach Taylor had not interfered. In just a few weeks she would have had everything worked out. DuBois Electronics would have been lifted from the ditch of failure and John would have understood her primary motivation was to enable the company to survive. CCC would have become the secondary company in the budding J.C. Martin empire, and linked with DuBois, both companies would have become stronger, dividing the computer distribution projects to the best advantage of each company. And she would have proved once and for all that she could handle the challenge.

Tossing her hair back from her perspiration-moistened face, Carol continued her aimless walk. Oh, God, she thought, how Alex Martin must be laughing, wherever he is. How he'd taunted her ambitions, laughed at her drive to succeed, to prove herself. How he'd ridiculed her every success until she could no longer stand the strain. He would have loved having the last laugh.

She'd divorced him just as quietly as they'd married. It had been a mistake from the beginning. She'd known it, but the word failure was not in her vocabulary. It had hurt. It had really hurt, even though what little love there had been between them had been killed early in their marriage by his taunting of her ambitions. And she'd sworn never to be hurt like that again.

But she'd wavered from her goal. Sidetracked by the handsome Cajun man who was her brother's savior. How ironic. Tears misted her eyes and she blinked them away stubbornly. How ironic that the first man in years to touch that frozen core of sensuality inside her was the very man who could destroy her.

"Excuse me," she said, bumping into someone. The sidewalks were crowded with tourists and local people. Night had fallen and the bright lights of New Orleans glowed against the night sky. But none of it really penetrated her consciousness.

She just wanted to forget everything—Zach, John, CCC, DuBois Electronics. All of it. She would take the first flight out of New Orleans, dissolve her association with CCC and cut her losses. When she felt ready, she would begin again somewhere far away from John and Zach and New Orleans.

Stepping to the curb, Carol waved down a passing taxi and slid inside. Closing her eyes, she surrendered momentarily to the weariness that suddenly engulfed her.

Back at the hotel, she rode the elevator to her floor, quickly unlocked the door and stepped inside. Carefully locking the door behind her, Carol felt safe for the first time this evening. She peeled off her clothes as she strode through to the bathroom to run a tubful of steaming water. After shaking in a packet of fragrant bath salts, she pinned her hair atop her head and sank tiredly into the water. After several minutes her taut muscles began to relax, and her tightly strung nerves began to loosen. Tears began to slide down her cheeks, and she didn't attempt to stifle them. If only she could make John realize how much she wanted to help. If only Zach would understand, give her the benefit of the doubt. If only... Famous words—if only.

Carol didn't know how long she'd been in the tub when a sound at the bathroom door brought her back from the dark hole of despair into which she'd allowed herself to sink. The water was now cool as it lapped gently against her breasts.

Zach stood in the doorway, one shoulder against the frame and one arm extended so his hand gripped the opposite frame. When she didn't respond to his appearance, he spoke in that rasping sensual tone that was so much a part of his personality.

"Are you all right?"

Carol continued to study him, her gaze moving over each detail of his face and body. His crisp black hair was windblown. His dark eyes were intently studying her in return. Somehow the lean features of his face seemed more compelling, and after having experienced its warm pressure, the firm line of his mouth more tantalizing. His body seemed more masculine, hard and unrelenting, and her own body responded automatically in spite of her mental lethargy.

"Should I be?"

Zach straightened and came fully into the room to sit on the edge of the tub. Leaning forward, his left forearm resting on his thigh, he trailed fingers in the water. Goose bumps rose on her skin.

"You're cold. Time to get out of there." He picked up the fluffy towel she had left lying on the floor. "Come on, stand up." Flicking the drain handle, he stood and held open the extra-large towel as the water began to drain from the tub.

It didn't matter now that Zach had been the catalyst for the destruction of her plans. Nothing mattered, really. Everything she'd ever wanted had been systematically torn asunder. Her marriage, her career, her self-confidence were all gone.

Stepping from the tub, Carol allowed Zach to wrap the towel about her. He tucked the end into the shadow between her breasts to secure it. She stood quietly as he patted her cold flesh dry with another towel.

"Come into the bedroom. I've ordered some coffee sent up. Do you have a warm robe?" He went to the closet and riffled through the clothes. "All I see are these filmy things. Beautiful but impractical." He finally abandoned his search and settled for a blanket he'd found on the top shelf.

Zach wrapped the blanket about Carol and settled her into a corner of the couch. At that moment a knock at the hotel room door signaled the arrival of the coffee he'd ordered. After tipping the man generously, Zach took charge of the tray of coffee and sandwiches. Zach poured a cup of the piping-hot brew and extended it toward her.

After a moment's hesitation, Carol took the cup and saucer. "What are you doing here, Zach?"

He settled himself into a chair opposite her, his cup and saucer balanced on his knee. "I was concerned about you."

"Why? You accomplished your mission. I'm humiliated and chastised. Put in my place, though it's not the 'place' I sought. You can return to your carefree life without further concern." A wry smile twisted her lips before failing completely. She sipped her coffee to fill the awkward moment.

Zach settled back in his chair, sipping at his own coffee, studying Carol. "It wasn't my intention to humiliate you. But I would like to understand why you planned so meticulously to destroy your own brother."

Anger flashed through her. "I didn't. He wouldn't have been 'destroyed.' I needed..." Carol controlled the anger commanding her tongue. "I only wanted to help, but John wouldn't let me in. I wanted to...share. I wanted only my part...."

"And taking the company to the brink of bankruptcy would have given you that?"

"Only to the brink, remember? No one else would have been hurt since it's a wholly owned company. In another week or so it would have been over. I would have spoken to John, explained my position and presented him with a proposition."

"What kind of proposition?"

His dark gaze upon her was unwavering. Once again Carol found her attention wandering. The cadence of his drawling speech made her senses quiver. It was hard to think clearly when he was near.

"A partnership," she finally said. "An equal partnership."

"You expected John to accept that?"

A half laugh accompanied her shift to a more comfortable position. "He wouldn't before. But I hoped he would...soon. I would have had proof of my talent in the way I'd handled CCC. He would have been forced to listen." Carol set her cup and saucer aside. "To John, I've always been just his little sister. He's always adopted the attitude of our father. Nothing short of this...shock treatment...would have made my point. I just didn't expect him to enlist such a strong...ally."

"I'm not against you."

"You're not for me." Carol slanted a look at Zach. "The little scene in John's office proved that."

With one hand Zach brushed idly at the denim of his formfitting jeans. "I was angry, and I think rightfully so. And a little disappointed. But—" he stood and eyed her intently "—I've done my job. I'll leave you now. Eat some of those sandwiches. I'll call you later."

Her gaze traveled slowly upward from his feet, stopping when it met his closed expression. "Why? I'm no longer a part of your job."

"In spite of what you've done, what you almost did, you intrigue me. And there are some questions I'd like answered."

Carol didn't respond to that, so without another word, Zach left the hotel room. It was a long time before Carol went to bed.

Chapter Six

When morning announced its arrival with a shaft of sunshine across her face, Carol rolled tiredly onto her side. After a few minutes she forced her unrested body to respond to a mental command to rise and face the day ahead.

Last night she'd avoided thinking about how she'd gotten into her predicament and how she'd get out of it, but she couldn't put it off any longer. Today she had to forgo emotion and deal with John and DuBois Electronics. It did not promise to be a pleasant day.

Glancing at the clock, Carol reached for the telephone at her bedside and dialed a number.

"Anita? Well, it's over. John knows about CCC and what I've been doing." She listened for a moment. "No. They don't know all the reasons. They've assumed the worst, of course. So as far as I'm concerned it's all finished. I'll be coming to the office before long and begin keeping an eye on things in person." After giving Anita a few instructions, Carol hung up the receiver.

Glancing about the room, Carol took a few more minutes to finish shedding the lethargy that had gripped her since returning to the hotel the night before.

Well, she told herself, you lost the gamble. It's time once again to cut your losses and salvage what you can. Crossing her arms, she rubbed her chilled flesh briskly.

Carol dressed in a navy-blue business suit, with a plain pale blue silk blouse. Crisp, cool, businesslike. Gold circle earrings and a simple gold watch completed the image of aloofness she sought. Not a trace of vulnerability remained.

Striding into the offices of CCC, Carol set herself to accomplish the tasks she'd set for today. She would reevaluate her relationship with John and try to keep Zach Taylor out of her thoughts.

"Anita, please bring the file on DuBois." Without hesitating, Carol strode on through the reception area and into her office. Glancing about quickly, she noted the slightly antiseptic decor, something that she had ignored until now simply because she was so rarely here.

"Before we get started, Anita, please order some plants for this office. Later today, I'll find some pictures and have them delivered for hanging."

"Then you're going to stay for a while?" Anita questioned.

"For now. Some things have changed, but for a few weeks I will be here to determine the future direction of CCC. There are also some personal problems involved.''

''Your brother?'' Anita didn't know all the details, but she was aware of who John was and of some of the reasons behind Carol's actions.

''Yes, though, today, I doubt he would recognize the relationship. He was naturally very upset when he found out about J. C. Martin.''

''I see.''

''I have a few letters to dictate, but first, if Zachary Taylor should call, I don't want to speak to him. Not for a few days, anyway. Put him off somehow, but gently.''

Though there was a question in her secretary's look, Carol ignored it and set immediately to work. An hour later, the letters dictated, she poured a cup of coffee and began going through the files on DuBois once again.

There had been no direct connection with the firm since her youth. Carol was certain Zach hadn't had a hint that she was J. C. Martin until he picked up the phone the night before. But, he had impeccable timing. Either that, or Anita had particularly bad timing.

Pushing back in her chair and sipping another cup of coffee, Carol considered the choices open to her. She could let the matter drop, go public in her competition with DuBois, discharge her own sources and deal openly or talk to John. The last choice was not a very attractive one. At the moment her brother would not be receptive to any discussion about anything she was connected with, much less the family business. Possibly the best thing to do was wait. And that was something Carol had difficulty in doing at the best of times.

After a light lunch of shrimp salad, which was brought in, Carol spent the afternoon reviewing the trends of CCC and rethinking her decision about the future of the company. At one time she'd considered a merger with DuBois. But now that was impossible. So would she keep CCC or cut her losses and leave town?

By four o'clock Carol had put into operation her decision to withdraw from the competition with DuBois. CCC would begin soliciting business to make money not to undermine DuBois. The sales staff would have to be enlarged, another project coordinator would probably have to be employed in the near future, stock would have to be upgraded and increased and that, too, would necessitate the hiring of more in-house personnel. But that could all wait until tomorrow.

Carol buzzed her secretary. When Anita entered the office, steno book in hand, Carol smiled. "I think I'll call it a day. Any calls I should see to before I leave?"

"No. People are accustomed to your absence, and you have the call-backs on your desk. Zach Taylor did call once, but I told him you were out of the office. He didn't try again, nor did he leave any message."

"Good," Carol said, though there was a little twinge of regret at his acceptance of her unavailability. "Then I'll go back to the hotel and do a little work there. I'll be in early tomorrow, but you don't have to be."

"Okay, but don't keep the nose to the grindstone too long." Anita grinned. "You'll get a blister."

"I'll remember that," Carol said with a smile.

In the car on the way to the hotel, Carol let her mind wander for the first time all day. It immediately conjured up the dark profile of Zach Taylor, and she recalled both the anger that had marked his face and the smiles that had occasionally lightened it. There had also been determination, the reflection of an attempt to understand her attitudes toward her brother. In the few times they had been together, a myriad of emotions had assailed her. They'd been most potent when she and Zach were on the bed in her hotel room before Anita called.

Several times during that night she had awakened with a start, her dreams tormented by the thought of Zach's mouth caressing her lips, trailing firm warm kisses down her body. Just thinking about his arms embracing her, the gentleness of his kiss as he had explored the warm recesses of her mouth, made her aware that it had been a long time since she'd really felt that close to anyone. But that was past. No longer would she have to be concerned about becoming too involved with Zach.

Back in her room, Carol set her briefcase down, stepped out of her shoes and curled her toes into the plush carpeting. Slipping out of her suit jacket, she ran slim fingers through her hair, loosening it to fall about her shoulders. She drew a deep breath. Mental fatigue was quickly overriding her decision to work this evening.

Finally abandoning herself to her weariness, Carol undressed. A few minutes later she was immersed in the tub and allowing the heat of perfumed bathwater to penetrate her stiff mucsles. Then, after patting dry, Carol slipped into a dark blue satin robe and belted it at the waist. The color deepened the shade of blue in her eyes and made her complexion seem even more creamy.

She returned to the sitting room of the suite and opened her briefcase. A knock at the door brought a frown to her face, and she dropped the lid on the case before striding to the door.

Zach Taylor stood outside. "Zach?" Puzzlement replaced aggravation in her face. "What are you doing here?"

"I tried calling you at work, but your very efficient secretary put me off. Said you were out of the office, but you weren't here, so I decided you'd told her to avoid me. Was I right?"

"Yes," she said, deciding the truth was the best course to take.

"Good." With one broad hand he pushed the door open and forced her to step aside.

When he stood in the center of the room, Carol turned. "Why 'good'?"

"Because that means I bother you."

"And that's good?"

"You bother me. I think we should find a mutual way of solving that problem. Like dinner tonight."

"I don't think that would be a good idea. Our relationship ended with the confrontation in John's office."

In spite of herself her gaze took in the jeans and the oxford-style shirt that Zach wore. As usual the jeans were comfortably worn and formfitting. The pale blue of his shirt, which was open at the neck, brought out the bronze of his skin. His hands rested on the unbelted waist of his jeans as he faced her from across the room.

"I don't think that's the case. At least, it isn't for me."

Carol stood up straighter, crossing her arms in front of her body as his intense gaze made her more than a little aware that beneath the soft folds of her robe she wore nothing. "That wasn't the message I got."

"I told you we'd see each other again."

"I assumed you meant for business."

"My business with you is completed. I saw John a little earlier and his sources tell him you've called off your dogs."

Her head tilted in question before she remembered to maintain a front of disinterested aloofness. It no longer mattered what John, or Zach, for that matter, did or didn't do. Or did it?

"John's sources or yours?"

A lifted eyebrow indicated her guess was correct. "It's only natural that my own ways of learning what I need to know are more...refined...than John's."

"I thought as much. I don't suppose you'd tell me what John plans to do now that I'm no longer tampering with the company."

"No. That's between you and your brother. I'm no longer on the case."

"Not even in an advisory capacity?"

His stance shifted and he continued to study her. "No. And that was John's decision, not mine. I suggested several avenues open to him in order to maintain the company and reestablish a solid financial base, but he has a new determination to do it alone. I think if his adversary had been anyone other than you, his decision would have been different."

"You don't agree with him?"

"I think there are facets of John's personality I hadn't discovered before. There's a kind of fanatic competitiveness as far as you're concerned that I hadn't seen before. I'm not sure that's good."

"I never thought it was."

"Was your relationship with John always so... competitive?"

"Always, and our father was usually at the root of it."

Zach shifted his stance restlessly. "Look, let's go somewhere for dinner. Somewhere we can talk."

Carol knew that was too dangerous. "I don't think there's anything for us to talk about."

"You're a stubborn lady," he commented. "There are some things I'd like to discuss."

"What?"

"I'd like to talk about you personally. Now that there's no conflict of interest, I'd like to explore our relationship."

"We don't have a relationship."

"Why are you so... skitterish... when it comes to personal relationships? It can't all stem from your father and John." When she didn't respond, Zach continued. "Come on, get dressed. You're tired, and you have to eat sometime. Why not eat with me? What could be the harm?"

Inside she knew there could be a lot of harm. There was the danger to her emotional equilibrium, as well as a residue of danger to her relationship with John, however strained that was right now. She had hopes of improving it in the future. But for once her emotional needs overshadowed the logic that had always ruled her life.

"All right. For just a while."

Alone in her bedroom, Carol spent a few moment steadying her nerves. Whenever Zach was around, she lost all the cool logic that was an almost innate part of her personality. In its place came an added awareness of her femininity, of her basically physical reaction to a potently masculine man. But it was more than that. He appealed to her on every level—intellectual and physical.

She was intrigued by him. While he appeared to have all the time in the world to consider a person or subject, in his active mind he was already solving problems. It was this ability to disarm his adversary, to reach into the concerns of others with sources readily available to him that made him so dangerous. His outward gentleness made her doubly wary of her reactions. He would take advantage of every crack in her armor.

Carol took a multicolored jersey wrap dress in muted shades of green and blue from the closet. It was casual but very seductive. The feminine side of her needed to respond to Zach's maleness, and though her logical mind argued against it, the female in her won.

Zach took her to a small restaurant. The atmosphere was uncomfortably intimate, but she said nothing, deciding instead that she could control the situation. After her disastrous relationship with Alex Martin, she'd always maintained control and kept herself heart-whole. Of course, she'd never been confronted with anyone like Zach Taylor.

While crossing the small dining room to their secluded table, Carol was well aware of the attention they attracted. Zach's Creole heritage was blatantly evident in his lean dark face and compact body. His well-coordinated movements and muscular physique were proof of his athletic prowess.

They were seated at a table placed in an alcove, and Carol continued to study her escort. She knew he must feel her gaze upon him, but he ignored it while choosing a predinner wine and glancing at the menu. When they'd ordered and the waiter had withdrawn, Zach asked, "Care to share your thoughts?" He relaxed back in his chair, his suit coat falling open to reveal his shirt stretched tautly across his chest. Her breath caught.

"I was just wondering who you are, what you are."

"I thought we covered that the first night we went out together."

"No, we covered the surface. You're a Creole and a Cajun, native to this area. Your college background and relationship to my brother are open knowledge. But who are you inside? I sense a very different kind of man than is obvious on the surface."

"Then I guess we both have the same questions. I know you're John's sister, that you're very competitive, very intelligent, accomplished and extremely goal oriented. But I don't know the inside of you, the whys and wherefores."

"That might be asking a little too much, Zach. I don't think I want you to know everything."

"But you want to know everything about me."

She allowed a small smile to curve her lips. "Then I guess that means we'll both be kept in the dark."

Zach leaned back in his chair while the waiter poured their wine.

"Why are you so afraid?" His voice was low, but she heard him clearly.

"Afraid? Me? I'm not afraid of anything." Mockery was evident in her response.

"You're hiding behind the name J. C. Martin. I'd like to know why."

"I wasn't aware that my business was of any consequence to you any longer."

"Come on. We're not in the boardroom. We don't have anyone auditing our every move and word. Level with me."

"Zach, it just doesn't matter anymore." Carol wished he would just leave the subject alone.

The tone of his voice changed subtly to one of persuasion. "This doesn't have anything to do with John or CCC. I would have been attracted to you wherever we met. Whatever business there was between us is finished. Tonight, I'd like to begin fresh with you."

Again they studied each other at length, measuring, weighing. Zach's gaze penetrated her facade of brittle professionalism. This man made her disregard as meaningless decisions that had once been made in a completely logical fashion. Why should anything Zach Taylor says or thinks make any difference, she argued to herself. But it did. Somehow it did.

"Why should I believe you?" she asked. "Maybe you're still trying to get information from me about my involvement with DuBois Electronics."

His mouth firmed. "You're determined to think of everything in terms of business. Is that why your marriage failed? Can't you be warm and honest in any way?"

Pain pierced her heart while anger flamed in her ice-blue eyes. Without a word she picked up her purse and prepared to leave the table. But when she stood, Zach's fingers swiftly encircled her wrist.

"Don't run, Carol. You've done far too much of that already."

His dark gaze held her. "What do you know?" Her voice was barely above a whisper, and her glance flicked suspiciously about the room, as if seeking some person to pin her accusations to.

"Nothing. But there are things I'd like to know. Yes, I know something about your stay at Gault and about CCC. But what I want to know can't be found in corporate files, in boardrooms or on financial statements. What I want to know can be found only in your most secret of secret places."

Artfully he used the seductive huskiness of his drawling voice, the compelling quality in his dark eyes. His fingers encircled her wrist loosely, but the chains of sensuality and passion about her heart were growing stronger by the moment.

Without exerting any real pressure, Zach persuaded Carol to resume her seat. Her knees suddenly weak, she slid into the chair and averted her gaze from him.

"Can we talk now?" His fingers slid from her wrist as it rested on the table.

"I don't know what you want."

"Talk to me. Just talk to me. About Joan Carol who was raised in a dominantly male household, who developed such strong competitive instincts she would ruin her own brother, who married..."

"You want to know quite a lot."

"I expect quite a lot."

Her gaze flickered upward to catch his and slid quickly away. "You are a determined man."

"When I see something I want."

She was hesitant, and it showed clearly in the breathiness of her question. "And you want me?"

"You know that. There's chemistry between us. This business with John doesn't change that. You can't run from it. I want to explore this, see where it might lead." He shifted in his chair, his drink untouched. She had nearly drained her glass, though, without really being aware of it. "I think you're afraid of intimacy, afraid of exposing your true thoughts and feelings. And I want to know why."

When she didn't respond, was incapable of responding for fear of crying, he went on. "I don't want to make a mistake with you, Carol. Too many mistakes have already been made—in people's understanding of you, in their opinions. I don't want to do that. I won't ask more than you can freely give."

Carol gathered her scattered resources. "A general exploration of senses that might last, say, a few weeks? Possibly a few months at the most?" She was glad to find her voice surprisingly steady. "My information indicates your relationships don't last long. You're a very eligible bachelor, and except for that one little mistake of marriage in your twenties, you've remained free. Why should I bother?"

"Your own investigative sources are very good."

"Probably as good as yours. Why is it that you haven't learned what you wanted through them?"

"What I want to know isn't available to them. Otherwise, I'd know already." When she only stared at the glass turning between her fingers on the table, Zach continued. "How can I convince you that my desire for you is emotional and intellectual as well as physical? The three are so intertwined that I can't separate them. Taking you to bed won't satisfy me, but knowing you, seeing inside your mind first, will."

"I don't know what to say."

"You will. Eventually."

It was a promise echoed in his dark eyes. She felt a tingle inside that indicated the signals she received were not only visual. There was an emotional bond being strengthened between them, and it made her afraid.

She was not a gambling woman. Always she depended upon her cool analytical mind. But this thing with Zach was enticingly dangerous. It was like walking a tightrope over a canyon of immeasurable depth. And the wire was already swinging beneath her unsteady steps. Still, some obscure goal enticed her, always just out of reach, always elusive. And she wanted to touch it.

Chapter Seven

They ate their meal without further conversation. But Carol knew Zach was only biding his time. She managed to eat most of the delicious food, though her appetite had been dulled. She tried to think through the situation, decide the best move to make. If she gave Zach enough information to satisfy his initial curiosity, maybe he would back off. There wasn't anything he could learn about Alex Martin or about Gault that he didn't already know. But there was always the possibility that he might stumble on that one individual who could point him in the right direction—a direction that would reveal too much and destroy her peace of mind.

"Are you finished playing with your food?" The question was accompanied by an enigmatic twist of his lips, as if he understood what was going on in her mind.

"Yes. I guess I lost my appetite."

"Anything to do with my questions?"

She conjured up a brief smile. "Why, whatever makes you think that?"

"You don't like being vulnerable. But a relationship like ours requires a certain amount of that."

"I can't envision you being vulnerable."

"Men are like women in that they're only as open and giving as they choose to be. The macho image demands that we not reveal secrets to just anyone."

She responded with a soft smile. "I can't see that sensitivity makes a man any less macho."

"I agree. The question is, why do you hide your responsiveness? You wrap yourself in a protective cloak." He leaned forward. "I want to get inside that cloak, wrap it about us both and keep the world outside." His voice dropped a tone to more carefully strum the strings of her sexual responsiveness. She felt as if he were actually touching her body with his voice, his gaze holding her captive as he looked into her very soul. "I'd like to hold you again, without having to subdue that fiery nature lurking beneath the icy exterior. I'd like to see you again, touch your warm body that responded so openly, so satisfyingly, and capture once again those soft lips."

He was leaning across the table, his dark gaze burning into her wide eyes. His voice was so low that she could hardly hear him, yet each word was burned into her mind. Her body grew warm, responding unconsciously to his verbal seduction. It seemed she could feel his hands on her again. Her skin thirsted for his touch.

"Please . . . Zach, please. Not here. You don't know. . . ."

"I know what you do to me. I know that I can't forget how we were together, how near I was to knowing you as few men have. I know that unfinished business came between us, but before that, it was going to be so good. And I want it. I want to hold you again without reservations, without anything between us. And it's what you want. I know that."

"No. It can't be...."

"Yes, it can," he rasped, his gaze upon her intensifying until she turned away.

She couldn't face him and lie anymore. He was right. She wanted him. She wanted to feast on what she had only tasted yesterday in his arms. But it was too dangerous. She couldn't afford to let him inside. It hurt too much to let people inside.

"No. Please, Zach. Just take me back to the hotel."

He sat without moving for a moment. Just when she thought he would continue his argument, he sat back and signaled for the waiter. In a very short time they were in his car and headed back to the hotel. The anger in him was obvious, and Carol carefully avoided looking at him, afraid to invoke that anger.

Zach insisted upon escorting her to the hotel room, though Carol assured him it wasn't necessary. He rode beside her in the elevator, still quiet. A nervousness alien to her nature pervaded her being.

At her door Zach plucked the key from her fingers and deftly inserted it in the lock. Swinging the door open, he followed her inside.

In the center of the room Carol faced him, her mouth open to tell him good-night. But before she could speak, his mouth covered hers, and with a masterful twist of his lips, gained entrance to the sweet recesses.

The room was dark as she hadn't had the opportunity to turn on a lamp. The draperies were closed. She could not see him, but he seemed to surround her. With unrelenting arms, he drew her to him, one hand sliding down her back to the curve of her waist to hold her to his hard frame. Through the thin fabric of her dress, Carol could feel the warmth of his skin. Her sensitive breasts were crushed against the hard wall of his chest, and the solid warmth of his thighs bore proof of his desire for her.

Automatically her hands rested on his shoulders. When his mouth left hers, she could feel his warm breath on her skin. With one finger, he threaded the length of her hair behind an ear and followed the touch with a series of warm firm kisses across her cheek, his tongue tracing the curve of her ear momentarily before his hand wound the length of her hair in his fist to capture her for the next series of mind-drugging kisses.

Her reasoning was gone, her logic destroyed. All that remained were her senses, which demanded the satisfaction of his touch, which craved his caresses and drove her to respond. Her hands slid along the strong slope of his shoulders to the curve of his neck and into the crisp length of his hair. Her fingers explored the contours of the back of his head where feathers of hair lay against his neck. With a thumb, she traced the curve of his ear and, following his example, breathed into it. She smiled at the small groan drawn from him.

His stance shifted so that she was drawn into the protection of his body. His fingers curled into the curve of her buttocks, and he drank from her deeply.

She responded, moving against him, her body needing to know intimately the contours of his hard frame.

The tie on her dress was loosened, and she was hardly aware when the soft fabric slipped from her shoulders and fell with a whispery sound to her feet.

"This is what I wanted," he whispered. "This is what I needed."

His hands followed the unveiled lines of her body. Carol had not worn a bra, her newly awakened sensuality demanding the feel of soft material against her responsive skin. Now his hands cupped the fullness of her breasts, his thumbs teasing the soft peaks. It seemed he knew exactly where to touch her, how to move against her, the perfect way to destroy the last walls she had clung to for protection.

The only thing standing against his full knowledge of her was the brief lace covering of her panties, but though his fingers teased the edge of the bikini-style covering, he ventured no further. And though her senses raged for satisfaction, Carol could appreciate that Zach would ask no more until he felt she was ready.

She slid her fingers inside the collar of his shirt, needing to touch him. The buttons down the front parted obligingly, and her hands moved over the crisp hair marking his hard dusky skin. She found the copper circles of his male nipples and caressed them until a rippling shiver was evidence of his reaction. A small satisfied smile curved her lips as she grew more bold in her exploration.

Pulling his shirttail free of his trousers, Zach invited her sensitive fingers to trace the ridged contours of his torso. Carol complied eagerly, sliding her palm across the flat plane of his stomach, over his ribs and around to the muscle-rippled flesh of his back. Boldly she slid long fingers inside the band of his jeans, tracing the curve of his spine into his firm buttocks. His hips rolled against her, and Carol ached with desire for him. Still, the gap would not be bridged.

"You're asking too much, baby, unless you're willing to give." Strain was evident in the huskiness of Zach's voice.

His mouth was hard and twisting when he took hers again, and his tongue was thrusting and demanding, telling her exactly what he wanted. Her nails scored his flesh in response, but he knew her . . . so well.

"I know, baby. I know." He whispered against her kiss-swollen mouth. "It's what we both want, but you still can't, can you?"

Carol couldn't answer. Her forehead rested against his breast, and her nerves were strung so tightly that her body quivered within his embrace. Her hands clenched in frustration, and yet she could be angry that he was making her know how much had been missing from her life for so long.

"I wish you hadn't said that." Her voice was so soft that he could hardly hear.

"Why? Don't you want to know how much I want you? Don't you want to know you can make me respond so easily? Can you deny any of it? Is that the way your marriage was conducted, with a distance between you and your husband? A platonic relationship?"

"No." The word was forced from her.

"Was it good between him and you? Tell me that. Was it?"

The pause lengthened significantly before she finally answered. "No."

"Why not?" His lips teased the corner of her mouth. "Is that why you're reluctant to enter a relationship with me? Has there never been anyone else?"

"No, there's never been anyone else."

"Why not? You're a highly responsive woman, no matter how hard you try to deny it. I touch you and you quiver. You're warm in my arms. You move against me in ways that twist my insides. Still you can't take that last step. Why?"

"Why, what?" she prevaricated, suddenly very aware of her nakedness—both physically and emotionally. Unconsciously her arms crossed in front of her, although it was so dark she could not see the expression on his face.

Zach's hands firmly gripped her upper arms as he held her a step away from him. "Don't play games with me, Carol. Games are for children and people who have never grown up. I want to know why you're afraid of physical intimacy, why you're unwilling to discuss in even the remotest fashion your marriage."

"It's not a part of our...relationship. It has nothing to do with you and me at this point."

Sensing he'd lost the initiative, Zach allowed his hands to slid down her arms before releasing her. He bent and picked up her dress from the floor, handing it to her. She could hear as well as sense Zach moving away from her as she slid her trembling arms into the sleeves of her dress. A dim light from a lamp Zach turned on lit the room as her clumsy fingers tied the fastening of her dress.

Zach stood across from her, intentionally taunting her as he freed the fastening of his jeans and thrust the tail of his shirt inside. His dark gaze held hers as he buttoned his pants and waited for her to break the silence.

"I think you'd better go, Zach. It's late, and I have to be at the office early tomorrow."

"Running again? It's a habit you'll have to break."

"Why?" The word seemed the only response she could make.

"Because our relationship is important...to me, at least. I want to be in your life, Carol. It's time you began to realize that I won't let you go this easily."

"How can you say that? We haven't known each other long enough for you to feel anything for me."

"Sometimes it doesn't require time in terms of days and hours. Sometimes it's a time of the spirit, an instantaneous knowing of each other." Zach took a step toward her, but when she would have moved back, he halted his advance. His gaze never left her. "My people are very intense. We play hard, we work hard. Our anger and sense of rightness are both very strong. I think you've wronged your brother, but I believe you did it in a spirit of rightness, motivated by something you won't discuss. Whether your motives were well-founded is not mine to judge and has nothing to do with how I feel about you personally."

"How can you separate the two? My competitive instincts are a part of my basic nature. You can't deny that."

"They are. And they reflect deep passions. Those of a very intense and strong woman. I like that. I would rather see those qualities channeled into support of me as your man than channeled against me. But that will come. I just want the opportunity to know more about you, to know what makes you tick. I think that's to be expected in light of the intensity of our sexual response to each other. You can't deny that. The body doesn't lie."

A light flush colored her cheeks, and his knowing smile made her feel chagrined that he was able to reach her so easily. "It was a learned response. I have been married, after all."

"Ah, yes, but you've admitted it was not a sexually compatible union. Was that why it didn't last? Or are you not ready to face that yet?" When she didn't respond, Zach continued. "You were married to the wrong man, Carol."

"Are you offering marriage?" Carol taunted, knowing the answer beforehand.

"Not yet. That would scare the hell out of you."

Carol blinked, surprised at his intuitiveness. "You're right," she admitted. "I won't make that mistake again."

"Never?"

"Never," she said, hoping it would put him off. But she was mistaken.

"Then that's something else I'll have to change."

"What are you talking about?"

"I've just proven to you that we are physically compatible. We are both goal-oriented, determined people."

"That doesn't sound like much fun . . . much too conventional," she teased.

He stepped nearer, and she held her ground, somehow no longer threatened by his physical proximity. "You don't know me well. You don't know how unconventional I can be under certain circumstances." When she flushed warmly, a smile curved his lips, but his eyes held a sultry warning that deepened the blush across her cheeks even more. "If you're questioning my fun-loving side, then tomorrow we'll go the park and I'll prove which side of my nature predominates. My philosophy is: Balance work with play, and you will be better able to enjoy the fruits of your labor. I'll pick you up immediately after work. You can change into a pair of jeans and get comfortable. I'll even buy you a hot dog for dinner.''

In spite of how intense the atmosphere of the room had been a few moments earlier, Carol's mouth curved in a smile at his bantering. She appreciated his decision not to continue badgering her about her marriage or Alex or, for that matter, about John or DuBois Electronics. These were all subjects she had not yet come to terms with, and she certainly wasn't ready to explain her feelings concerning them to Zach.

With DuBois Electronics constantly intruding on her thoughts, she felt drained and exhausted after just a normal work day. But when she arrived at the hotel, her senses were humming, and she felt restless. Quickly showering, Carol slipped into the jeans she had purchased at noon and the blue plaid shirt that had been another purchase from her brief shopping expedition.

When Zach's knock came at the door, she was ready. Swinging the door open, she found her outfit almost matched his, and both of them grinned widely.

"You see," Zach said as he stepped inside, "we're much more alike than you thought."

"Probably more so than I care to consider," she returned, stepping away from him. Just the sight of him stirred her senses, and she didn't welcome the feeling.

"That's a revealing statement. Care to expand on it?"

"No. You're far too self-confident as it is. I'd like to keep a few things to myself."

"Only for a little while, Carol. Only for a little while."

The teasing smile was gone from his face when Carol looked up at Zach. She knew for certain that he had not relented one whit in his determination to dip into the secret wells of her very being. She shivered but she closed the door on those fears for this evening. For tonight, she just wanted to be free of her problems and enjoy being with Zach. And while she knew that was a dangerous precedent to set, she did it all the same, without really knowing why it was so important.

Zach drove toward uptown New Orleans, and soon Carol realized they were approaching Audubon Park, which was near the campuses of Tulane and Loyola universities. The park itself covered 315 acres between the Mississippi River and St. Charles Avenue. It included a zoo, a golf course and an outdoor swimming pool. One of the unique features of the park was a man-made hill that was built originally to show the children of the flat city of New Orleans what a hill looked like. The two universities faced the entrance to the park, which was on St. Charles Avenue.

As Zach drove into the parking area, Carol glanced about, awakening memories. "Did you spend much time here while in college?"

"Sure, there are some great places to take girls late in the evening."

Carol slanted a glance at Zach to see if he was teasing, and her mouth turned up at one corner when she caught his smile. "I know you're teasing, but I imagine that statement is not far from the truth. I remember you then, and I also remember there was a different girl on your arm every time I saw you.''

"Ah, but you saw me only once.''

"No, I saw you more than that. But you didn't see me. I was very careful about that.'' As soon as she'd said it, Carol wished the words back. They would be another tool to use against her.

"Oh? And where did you see me?'' A teasing glint flashed in his dark eyes.

Caught, Carol told him. "Oh, at various events. I could come because John was there, and of course there was graduation.''

"I wish I'd known. Look at the time we wasted.''

"You weren't very interested in someone like me then. I was too dull.''

"You make me sound like a very shallow person.''

"Not at all. Merely typical. I was odd man out, so to speak. Too dedicated to succeeding, too intense and rather hostile.'' She stared out the window in order to avoid meeting his questioning look. "I haven't changed much, but you have. You've matured, become certain of your goals, and you've reached them. I wish John could do that.''

"You love him very much, don't you?'' He spoke cautiously.

"Yes. Does that surprise you?''

"In a way. You said you wanted him to find his own place in DuBois Electronics, but I'm afraid I discounted that in light of your actions. I'm sure he's done the same thing.''

Surprised at the moistness in her eyes, Carol blinked and forcibly steadied her voice. "Yes, he probably has. As usual, I've made poor choices in my personal relationships. It seems to be a fatal flaw in my character.''

His hand on her shoulder made her flinch, but he drew her to him relentlessly. His arm about her was warm and comforting. ''I'm here to help, if you'll let me.''

''It's too late. And I've never been good at asking for help.''

''Have you needed to very often?''

She almost didn't answer, but something inside her once again compelled emotion to rule over logic. ''I've needed help, but no one was there for me. But I don't need anyone now. I've learned that being alone is best.''

''It's not. It may be safest, but it's not the best. Having someone to share the failures and triumphs, that's the best.''

''I wouldn't know.'' Her voice was muffled as she spoke against his chest.

''Didn't your husband do that for you? Didn't he share your happiness, your sorrows? Couldn't you trust him enough to allow him that privilege?''

''Privilege? He wouldn't have considered it a privilege.'' Bitterness laced her words. ''All he knew was taking and ridiculing and taunting. I was never enough for him. The things I needed were what tore us apart in the end, and there was nothing I could do about it.''

''What did you need?''

Carol hesitated, needing to talk, afraid to let him see inside her. ''It's easier to tell you what he wanted. He wanted a woman who would do exactly what he demanded without question. A woman with no individual goals, who'd wait on him with total dedication. He wanted the perfect combination of a woman from that saying." Carol pulled back, gathering her emotions and enveloping them inside for protection. "What's that old joke? I've found the perfect woman. Who could ask for anything more? She's deaf and dumb and oversexed and runs a liquor store." Carol gazed out the window, willing herself back to composure.

But Zach would have none of it and pulled her against him. "Well, you're certainly not deaf and dumb. Do you own a liquor store?"

Zach's teasing forced Carol to turn around and look at him. Instead of the rejection she'd expected, there was a perfectly natural smile curving his lips. For a moment she just stared, overwhelmed by his acceptance of her and his ability to make her feel so very special.

"No," she said slowly. "A liquor store isn't among my holdings. The third item doesn't match either."

He grinned at her. "I'll have to have that proven. From the samples I've tasted, that third area might be a winner."

Finally an answering smile teased Carol's lips. Her tense nerves began to relax and it seemed she could breathe again after a long time. Zach Taylor was a very special man. And she didn't want to lose him.

"Well, now that we've settled that," Zach said, "let's go for a walk. When is the last time you spent time in a zoo?"

Carol joined him outside the car. "Corporately speaking, already today." Her laughter joined his and she felt wonderfully comfortable when Zach's arm slipped about her shoulders while he strolled beside her.

"Well, let's see what kind of personalities we can see here. There is, of course, the pompous buffoon." He gestured toward the elephant house. "And the junior executives. They tend to swing from chandeliers and scrape and bow at the slightest whim in order to get attention." They were passing the monkey cages.

The narration continued through the zoo. The ostriches were tagged as members of a board of directors, often burying their heads in the sand in order not to recognize the trials of running a business in an economically vacillating world. They passed flamingos that were standing first on one foot and then the other. They were either clients, changing their minds at every whim, or office clerks, afraid of making a mistake. Sea turtles were the ponderous oldsters in any corporation who continually say, "But we've never done it that way before." The big cats were naturally the predatory heads of corporations, the movers and shakers in any area.

True to his word, Zach treated her to a hot dog dripping with mustard, ketchup and relish from a street vendor's cart. Wiping her stained fingers on napkins while he bought ice cream, Carol marveled at the relaxed feeling inside her. It had been a long time since she'd been able to just enjoy being with a man without pressures of one kind or another preying on her. In her experience men wanted one of two things— a romp in bed without commitment or a hand up in business in some way. She'd always rejected both sorts of propositions, but with Zach it was different. And she was still afraid of how that difference would affect her.

Chapter Eight

It was rather sad that it was all over. She was now totally and irrevocably disconnected from DuBois. Trying to take over had been a move motivated by desperation—a move that, it turned out, had not been wise. She had totally destroyed any possibility of becoming a part of the family business, and probably any hope of reestablishing a relationship with her brother along with it.

Then there was the relationship between herself and Zach. She hated the feeling that Zach had taken her on as a *project*. Was he truly interested in her now, or was his attention only the residue of his commitment to John? Very often, when his probing questions went too deep, she wondered if he was just indulging in a little amateur psychology.

Carol sat at her desk, the work before her forgotten. It was evening, long past quitting time. The offices were quiet. Everyone had gone home long ago.

It was the time of day she hated, that limbo time between the work day and the evening when all she could
do was go to her hotel, order dinner from room service and watch the early news. Later, she could work
some more, bury her thoughts in the intricacies of
business. When bedtime finally came, she would surrender to sleep only to wake up the next morning anx-
ious to return to the office.

It had always been that way. Even in college she had
filled every minute of her time with classes and studying. She had often been teased about burying her nose
in books, but it filled the time. Maybe she and John
hadn't been so very different after all.

Carol had always been interested in the family
business, drinking in her father's dinner table talk that
had been directed toward John. Whenever she ventured an opinion or question, it was always dismissed
and she'd early grown to resent her exclusion.

In college John's desire had been to teach, while
Carol had striven for a place in the business world. It
hadn't been easy. In the first place, she was female. An
added burden was that she was classically blue-eyed
and blond, slim and feminine in appearance. In the
career she chose, these definitely were not assets. It
seemed the Southern-gentleman syndrome predomi-
nated at all corporate interviews on campus, and when
she actively sought interviews outside those scheduled
by the school, the reception was even more cool.

In spite of her academic record and ability to sell
herself, other factors seemed to get in the way. The
central question seemed to be whether she planned to
marry and have children, which would indicate a
short-term commitment to the corporation and that all
the money spent in training her would be wasted. Well,

she had solved that problem. She had married, but it hadn't improved the situation.

A brief knock on her open office door jerked her from her reverie. Zach stood in the doorway.

"Zach! How did you get in?"

"A name has certain power. What are you doing here so late? I called the hotel, and when you weren't there, I assumed you'd be working. It seems a kind of balm for you, an escape."

She sat up straighter. "A balm? That sounds like I have an injury to heal."

"Don't you? Isn't that why you bury yourself in work? Why you set up such an elaborate plan to make inroads into DuBois?" At her wary look, he continued, "Yes, I know just how much trouble you went to to avoid being uncovered. It was quite clever and complicated. You're a highly intelligent woman, Carol. I just wish you'd use some of that intelligence to make friends with your brother."

"Make friends? That's a strange term. Anyway, I don't think John wants that. When I tried to contact him, there was definitely coldness in his refusal to see me. Now his secretary makes excuses—he's in a meeting, he's out of the office."

Zach lounged in the doorway, his casual clothes evidence that he had already been home to change. "And that bothers you." It was not a question, but a statement indicating understanding.

Carol stood and began to shuffle files, sliding papers inside with intense concentration. "Yes, it bothers me. I never wanted a permanent rift between us. I understood that he would be upset when he learned what I'd done, but I'd hoped we'd be settled in and working together by that time. I never wanted him hurt by any of it. That's the truth.''

"I accept that. But I was working on a consulting basis for John. My first allegiance was to him.''

"And what about now? Where do your interests lie now?'' She had to ask the question although she wasn't certain she wanted to hear the answer.

"If I told you, would you believe me?''

Her hands halted in their task as she looked up. "I'm not sure.''

"Would you if I hadn't been working for your brother but operating as an independent company in which CCC was interested?''

It was something she had considered, given the circumstances of their meeting at the historical society charity ball. She had approached him deliberately. It had been a dangerous thing to do, but she'd counted on him not recognizing her at first and depended heavily on the intuition that even if he was working for John, he would have no idea of her connection with the J. C. Martin he sought. She had covered her tracks well, but as it had turned out, not quite well enough.

"I'm not sure. But that question is moot now, isn't it? The damage is done.''

"Have you eaten yet?'' he asked, changing the subject abruptly.

Glancing automatically at her watch, Carol was surprised to see it was almost eight o'clock. "No...I totally forgot about the time.''

"Then will you have dinner with me at my home?''

Her glance flicked to him and then away as she plucked her purse from the bottom drawer of her desk. "You've planned something?''

"Yes," he admitted, "I did, hoping you would join me."

"All right." He seemed almost surprised at her acceptance.

In just a few minutes Carol was in Zach's car, and he was driving toward the Garden District. It was an area settled by Americans who came to New Orleans after the Louisiana purchase in 1803. Some of the city's finest homes stood in the tree- and flower-filled area, which bordered on St. Charles Avenue. Many of the homes had fragrant gardens shaded by magnolias, oaks and other graceful trees. Carol knew that the homes in the Garden District were known for their wide porches and spacious rooms. They'd been built in a combination of Greek and other classical styles. When she stepped inside Zach's home, she found it was a good example of the fine old established homes of the area.

"How long has your family lived here?" Carol asked as Zach took her jacket.

She had worn a classically tailored business suit in charcoal gray, with a pearl-white blouse. The suit skirt was pencil thin, with a slash in the front seam that revealed tantalizing glimpses of her inner leg when she walked. In spite of the heat of the approaching summer she'd worn a blouse with long sleeves. It sported a soft bow at the throat. She had pulled her hair back into a chignon at the nape of her neck, revealing the strong lines of her face.

"My parents were able to move into this house when I was twelve. They had worked very hard, advancing an interest my grandparents had started, combining it with an inheritance my mother received from her parents. They were hardworking people, and fortunately, they were able to enjoy the fruits of their labor for many years before their deaths.''

''But you said your family had been in New Orleans for many generations?''

Zach directed her into a spacious living room. Cream painted woodwork and matching walls gave a feeling of open airiness that contrasted pleasantly with the humid heat of Louisiana. An evening breeze was moving through the open French doors, which led onto a patio. The yard was manicured. Flowers bloomed in profusion, sending their fragrance into the house. The trees were big and old, conveying a sense of establishment.

Zach answered her question as he poured a glass of wine for each of them. ''They have been, but not in the Garden District. My grandmother's house was in Algiers.''

Carol knew that Algiers was an area of New Orleans on the south side of the river. It was necessary to drive over the Greater New Orleans Bridge to get there.

''The house was modest. But you have to understand that even if my grandparents had been very wealthy they would never have moved. They were not interested in living in the 'right' house, doing the 'right' things. They were only interested in being comfortable and happy. And I'm glad they were.''

Carol curled into a corner of the couch, accepting the glass of wine Zach handed her before he claimed the opposite end of the sofa. ''Then why do you live in this large house alone? Why did your parents live here?''

''Because they enjoyed this. And I live here for the same reason. This is my home. It has been for a good many years. You'll find that I live my life as I see best, not for anyone else."

"Very noble," Carol commented dryly, sipping her wine again.

"What about your parents? What were they like?"

A smile curved her lips but it never reached her eyes. "Competitive, brash, conscious of approval and appearances, determined to be someone. That was my father, and he was the dominant parent. If Mother had lived, it wouldn't have been much different."

"I see. Sounds like you and John sort of got lost in the drive for achievement. Is that why you are so...goal oriented, for lack of a better phrase?"

"Playing amateur psychologist doesn't suit you, Zachary." She slanted a glance at him. He was probing again, and she didn't like it.

"Evasion doesn't suit you, Joan Carol," he teased. "Come with me while I see to the steaks. I've had them marinating for an hour, and they should be just right for grilling."

She followed him toward the back of the house, where a large patio opened off the spacious kitchen. Casually, Zach checked the grill, which was nearly ready for the steaks, then lifted two large sirloins out of the pan in which they had been marinating.

"Whew!" Carol commented, seeing the size of the pieces of meat. "I'll never get around that!"

"Trust me. It's delicious. You can do the salad. The vegetables are in the refrigerator."

Carol did as he suggested while Zach put the meat on to grill. Taking lettuce, tomatoes, onions, radishes, along with anything else she could find, she rolled up her sleeves and began searching through drawers for a knife. In just a few moments she was busily putting together a masterpiece of fresh green salad. The aroma of meat and spices and charcoal wafted in through the door. It was a totally domestic scene, and Carol felt a little out of place in it.

"I'll set the table while you finish that," Zach said.

"Fine. You do have some salad dressing, don't you? I told you I'm not too domestic. Simple things only."

"I like simplicity. It's when things get too complicated that I begin to worry."

Her hands halted in their task. "You're referring to the DuBois-CCC business?"

"Only in a remote way. I think it applies to a more personal situation. I think you've entangled yourself in a maze of agonies that you're having difficulty sorting out."

"And I think your degree is not in psychology. Leave it alone, Zach. I have to do things in my own way."

"I'd like to help."

He was leaning against the refrigerator, his gaze upon her, compelling Carol to face him. But she resisted. "You've helped enough. That's part of my problem."

"What is? The fact that we're attracted to each other? Does that concern you?"

"Yes, but I don't want to analyze it now." She turned to him then, the paring knife still in her hand. "I just want to have a nice evening. I want to spend it here in this lovely house. Eat some of that delicious steak and relax. I need that, Zach. Please don't spoil it."

Something moved behind his dark eyes. "All right. For this evening I won't pressure you. I'll go check on the steak. There's dressing in the refrigerator. Something I mixed up earlier.'' A teasing glint replaced the serious expression on his face, and she relaxed perceptibly.

''You're a man of many talents, Zachary Taylor,'' she rejoined, thankful that the atmosphere had lightened.

Zach went out to turn the steaks and Carol finished the salad. In a short time they were seated across the table from each other, enjoying the delicious product of their joint effort. When Carol couldn't eat another bite, Zach suggested they adjourn to the living room for coffee.

Seated again on the couch, Carol glanced about the room with interest, taking in the decor, colors, pictures. ''This is a lovely home. Has it changed any since your parents were alive?''

''A little, but I've kept it basically the same.''

Zach joined her on the couch. The evening was warm but not uncomfortably so. The light breeze stirred the filmy curtains at the windows. A small lamp provided the only light in the room, and the shadows made their proximity intimate and warm. Carol shivered, realizing how her senses were stirred by just being with Zach.

She pushed away the dangerous feeling of intimacy, which was eroding her determination to remain untouched by him in any way. ''Due to your interest in preserving historical sites?'' she suggested, sipping at her coffee, hoping she hadn't paused too long.

''In a manner of speaking. But more because I like it as it is, and…sometime I may decide to marry, and my wife may want to decorate it to her taste.''

For some reason her throat closed at the thought of him marrying. "You were married before. Why didn't it work?"

His eyes took on a faraway look, as if he was traveling back to a time he'd tried to forget. "Her name was Stacy Parker. We met in college, had a grand affair and made the mistake of making it permanent. I was very involved with my family's business and restless to a certain degree. I was toying with the idea of starting my own company. She thought that was ridiculous. Travel and excitement were more her idea of the perfect life-style.

"She couldn't understand why I wanted to continue working just to achieve things my parents had already given me—money, success, a name, stature in the community. And I couldn't seem to live the life she wanted. The constant round of parties began to bore me, and soon we were going our separate ways while living in the same house. It wasn't very long before we both decided that it was a ridiculous situation and agreed to a divorce. It was amiable. We see each other occasionally, exchange Christmas cards. Fortunately the pain faded quickly, and we're both better off for having realized our mistake and not compounding it by staying together." Zach set his cup and saucer on the floor beside the couch. "How about you? What happened?"

Darn, she thought. He is a stubborn man. "It's not an experience I can remember with anything near the acceptance you have of your situation." She shifted her position. "I'd rather hear about your company."

"Changing the subject subtly is not your strong point, is it?"

"Nope." She smiled. "But persistence is yours."

"You'll have to talk about it sometime."

"You've said that before, but I don't agree. Our relationship is limited to my stay in New Orleans. And I don't expect that to be very long."

"Planning on leaving CCC? I thought you might stay in New Orleans. After all, this is your hometown and your roots are here."

"Not very strong ones, Zach. Not roots like you have here in this house, in your family. I envy you that. And yet, it wouldn't work for me."

"You don't think so? It's what you want, isn't it? A place to belong, someone to come home to, someone to share your life with?" His words were low and penetrating, like sharp little arrows hitting the soft core of her heart.

Her answer was a long time in coming as she finally faced the truth. "Yes, I guess it is, though at any other time I would have denied it. Being here tonight, in this house, seeing what I've missed, makes me recognize a few things. I don't know what it is, but this house conjures up dreams I had as a child, fantasies I had as a young woman. But it's too late. Too late." She stood and walked to the open French doors to stare out into the darkness.

There was the faint sound of his rising, and she sensed Zach come up behind her. He didn't touch her, but he was there, and she wished he would put his arms about her and tell her everything would be all right. In the morning she wouldn't believe it, but tonight it was very tempting to lean back against him and surrender to his strength and to the care he constantly exhibited.

"Is it really too late?" His voice was low and plucked at the already sensitive strings of her heart.

"You asked about my marriage. Alex Martin was his name. A man I met my last year of college, just before I got my degree. He was in insurance, moderately successful, extremely flattering. He was fun, effusive, generous. Always the life of the party. When I got my job with Gault he was pleased. We married then, and I thought everything would be wonderful."

"What happened?" Zach softly prompted.

With her arms crossed defensively in front of her, Carol allowed her head to rest against the door frame. She stared out into the night, trying to detach herself in some way from the pain of revealing her own failure as a wife, as a woman.

"My job was time- and energy-consuming. I knew it would be when I took it. Alex would have preferred me to stay at home but he accepted my desire to work. He hadn't realized, however, how dedicated I was, and he resented the time I spent at Gault. His own hours were erratic. Often he worked late at night. And when he was home, he wanted me there with him. But I had to be at the office early.

"That conflict was just the beginning. I would work late because he was seldom home in the evenings, and sometimes I'd work weekends, too. When a promotion came up he wasn't pleased when I received it because it made him feel I was passing him, that while his own career remained static, I was upwardly mobile.

"But I took the promotion. After all, it was what I'd worked for, and I deserved it. The company was in better shape than ever, due in a large part to my efforts, and I was proud of that. But Alex resented my accomplishments.

"Very soon he started to complain. I felt guilty and tried to do what he wanted. I came home at five, prepared dinner, spent the evening at home. But Alex was seldom there. I spent the weekends at the house, but he'd be working. It was only later that I learned he hadn't been working. His good-time-Charlie act extended to a number of appearances with women friends in public. All the time he was castigating me for being unwomanly, for not fulfilling my obligations at home, for emasculating him publicly by being successful while his career remained static, he was spending his time with various women whose talents were not exactly centered in the kitchen.'' Bitterness tinged her words and tears of defeat stung her eyes.

"What did you do?"

Even white teeth savaged her lower lip. "I divorced him quietly."

"He didn't contest it?"

"He couldn't afford to. He was spending all his money on fun and games. My check paid for the house, furniture and cars. So I moved out, gave the house to him as a settlement and took my own apartment. A quick trip out of the country, and I was quietly divorced."

Zach finally spoke up. "While I was working with John, we tried to find out who J. C. Martin was. There was no record at all. When I shifted to trying to learn something about you, I ran into a stone wall. I didn't find any record of marriage or divorce. Now I know why."

"We went to Texas to get married. I didn't know why, but I suspected later it was because he didn't want the female population of Shreveport knowing anything about the marriage. He was very willing for me to get the divorce in a quiet manner, too."

"Why was that?"

"Because while a marriage might make him secure, it would also limit some of his...activities," she stated baldly.

"What a louse," Zach commented, studying her intently.

Stiffening her resolve to finish what she'd started, Carol faced him. "Standing before you is a complete fool. Alex learned about my family, thought he could wend his way into the family business, not realizing I could be no help in that way. When he realized how things stood between me and my family, we were already married."

"So when did you learn all this?"

"Alex contacted me a year after we were divorced. He needed money and thought he could blackmail me into giving him a few thousand dollars. Apparently he had thrown off all pretense of working in insurance, though he had a good future there at one time. He had gambled a little too heavily on one of his lady friends being discreet. Her husband, who wielded considerable power, apparently suspected something and Alex opted for getting out of town. Unfortunately he was caught a little short in the cash department. He must have been desperate to contact me."

Carol delivered the information in a clipped tone. By telling Zach the story, she would put an end to his questions. He wouldn't want her once it was all said.

"I thought it wise to do a little investigating into just who and what Alex Martin was and had been, in case this sort of thing cropped up again. The man I hired was very good. I only wished I had thought of it before the whole mess happened." She shrugged, drawing herself back to the present. "In any event, I learned the extent of my foolishness and was glad to be out of it virtually unscathed. End of story.''

Zach's dark gaze moved over her closed face, attempting to penetrate the mask that was now firmly in place. ''Somehow I don't think it was that simple.'' The backs of his fingers caressed her cheeks before moving down the length of her neck to gently massage her stiff shoulders. Unrelentingly he drew her to him and folded her into his arms, pressing her head against his chest.

She came almost willingly, clinging to her last vestiges of pride, which told her she should not allow Zach to comfort her. She was too susceptible to his seduction.

''I've never told anyone that before. I never wanted to. It was too humiliating,'' she whispered, basically to herself. But Zach heard her.

''I know, and I'm glad it was me you trusted enough to share it with. Pain is lessened when two people carry it.''

''I don't understand that.''

His fingers gently loosened the pins in her hair, and he let the silken strands fall across the back of his hand. With gentle pressure, he massaged the tense cords in her neck, pressing her into him comfortingly.

''It's simple. When you carry all that guilt and pain yourself, no one has the opportunity to make you realize you're not the only person in the world to make a mistake. Not the only woman to marry the wrong man or to be duped by a shyster. Certainly you should have known better, but you were looking out from the heart. That often clouds the vision. Alex Martin was more guilty in dealing so dishonestly with you. He knew exactly what he was doing. Whatever he said or did after you were married can be discounted as jealousy, anger, his need to strike out at someone who was a better person than he could ever hope to be.''

Her arms crept about his waist as she surrendered a little to the need to hold him. "You're good for my ego, Zachary Taylor.''

His embrace tightened, and his words were breathed into her hair. "I could be good for you in other ways, too.''

Chapter Nine

Her body stiffened and she gazed up into Zach's face. Softness was replaced with brittleness when she finally responded. "So, this was a seduction scene after all. I'm sorry. That's not my game."

"Carol, don't pull away from me."

"I think it's time I left. Your curiosity has been satisfied. You know the whole story. Your job is complete. I'm sure John will give you a generous bonus."

The warmth was gone from his face, and his gentle embrace tightened. He shook her gently but firmly. "Now wait just a minute! That wasn't what this was about. Besides, my connection with John was terminated the day I learned you were behind CCC and you stopped interfering in DuBois Electronics. Why can't you believe that?"

Fire flashed in her blue eyes but she was cold as ice inside. Her fists were clenched against his chest as Zach held her immobile. "Because men are only interested in J. C. Martin, not the woman behind the name!'' she shouted, and jerked in his grip.

Zach was relentless. ''You can't believe that of me! You can't look in the mirror every morning and believe that no man has ever been attracted by the image you see there. You're a beautiful woman, Carol, and you're bright and articulate and interesting. And no real man can fail to be intrigued by that certain coolness, that aloofness that is so much a part of the public image you've created.'' His voice calmed but he continued to hold her. ''I got a taste of a different kind of woman the other evening, and it made me hungry for more. I want to know your responses, I want to feel your body next to mine, touch your satin skin.'' His voice was silky and seductive and he drew her slowly back into his embrace. ''I want to hold you and kiss you and make love to you.''

''The fantasy is better than reality, Zach. Let me go.'' But he would not allow her to pull from his grasp.

''Why, Carol? Why do you think so little of yourself...?'' Sudden understanding dawned. ''Alex Martin made you believe you aren't a responsive woman, a woman capable of giving fulfillment or achieving it. You said that, and I didn't believe it or understand the complexity of your statement.'' He pulled her into his arms, holding her stiff body close. ''I can't believe a man who cared anything about you could have done that. How could you continue to believe it when you learned what kind of man he really was?''

She didn't respond but he felt her body begin to relax a little. His hands moved over her back and she felt the warmth through the silkiness of her thin blouse. Carol shifted her stance, moving unconsciously against him. His response was immediate and obvious. When she stiffened again in his arms a light chuckle rumbled in his chest.

"See there? See what you do to me and how easily?" He began to plant light kisses at her hairline, continuing to caress her body in ever-increasing circles of pleasure.

Without really meaning to, she lifted her face to coax his kisses onto her mouth. Readily he responded, his firm lips moving across hers to accept the first hint of initiation on her part. Her arms moved around his waist and her head rested easily against him as Zach explored the warm recesses of her mouth. She responded hungrily.

Her hands slid beneath his shirt to encounter the solid warmth of his body. Zach shifted his stance just enough to allow himself access to the buttons of her blouse and slipped them free. When his hand covered the width of her stomach above her waist she moved automatically against him, seeking him.

Sliding her hands up his torso, Carol's fingers moved beneath the collar of his shirt. Following his example, she soon loosened the buttons of his shirt, and her fingers tangled in the thick mat of dark hair on his chest. His groan of pleasure when she touched him fed her need to explore him.

In one swift movement, Zach bent and picked Carol up, cradling her against him easily. Startled, she blinked her eyes wide open and looked at him with uncertainty even as her arms went about his neck.

"Don't worry, honey. This won't go any further than you want it to. I just want to hold you for a while."

Without another word, he took her silence as acceptance. In a moment he was striding up the curving stairway to the second floor of the quiet house. Shouldering open the second door on the left, Zach entered the darkened room, which was obviously his bedroom.

Gently he laid Carol in the center of his large bed. When Zach moved away from her to reach for the lamp, her hand on his arm halted the movement.

"Please, leave it."

"I want to see you. I want to see all of you."

"Please." She hardly recognized her own voice, it was so . . . so uncertain.

"All right. This time. But another time I will indulge myself." He came back to the bed and relaxed alongside her. His fingers traced the contours of her face. Her body lay rigid, and Carol strove to close her mind to the fears raging inside.

"It isn't necessary," she whispered.

"It is for me. It's the difference between sex and making love. I want to make love to you." He accompanied his words with light tempting kisses, moving slowly from the feathers of hair at her temple to finally caress her lips with his.

Almost tentatively her hands moved up the solid length of his arms and over the curve of his shoulder, then up the column of his neck to thread through his hair and draw his face to her. When his mouth covered hers again, she felt as if something were breaking loose inside her and she struggled to free herself from his embrace.

For a long moment Carol stared up at Zach. He saw her doubt reflected in her eyes. And in that long moment he seemed to struggle to regain some control of himself.

His eyes closed and he drew a long tortured breath. "I want to love you, Carol. I want to show you what it can be."

"Zach . . . I'm not . . ."

"Let me make you certain. Let me . . ."

"No," she whispered. "I can't." The words seemed dragged from her constricted throat. "I can't until I'm certain I'm really ready. . . ."

Momentarily his forehead rested against hers. His body was tense as he fought for control over the passion they'd both had a part in building. Then Zach moved away and lay beside her. Words were not spoken. There were none that could be said.

I've lost him, Carol thought. I've been a fool again.

Carol awoke slowly, wonderingly, aware of a weight across her stomach and an unaccustomed warmth at her side. The room was still dark, and she could see little of it. But when she turned her head, the moonlight revealed the sleeping features of Zachary Taylor.

A kind of panic gripped her. Some of her emotion must have been conveyed to Zach because he stirred in his sleep, his eyes opening slowly to meet her wide-eyed gaze. Sensing her withdrawal, he rose on one elbow, without moving his arm that lay across her.

"It's all right, Carol. Nothing happened. . . .and nothing will until you're very certain of what you want." Almost idly his hand came up to thread the hair back from her face and secure it behind her ear. He was giving her time—time to think, time to control her reactions. "It can work no other way. You have to want me as much as I want you."

Her mouth twisted in response, and her gaze slid away from his. "Right. Now you'd better take me back to the hotel."

His arm tightened around her. "I want you to stay with me. I want to wake up with you like this every morning."

The tone of his words arrested her movement and drew her gaze back to his. "Why?"

"Because I know something of what goes on inside your head now, and I want to know more. If I let you go, you'll convince yourself that this—" he gestured from himself to her "—meant nothing. We were so close last night. What I feel with you, I want to know every day, and every hour. I want to love you. I want to reach inside and tear out all those doubts and fears you have and convince you that Alex Martin was the fool. Not you. I can give you all the things you want, if you'll only let me."

"And what is that?" she asked warily.

"Love, acceptance, security, happiness . . . children, a home."

"Why would you want to do that?"

"Because you're what I've been looking for, for a long time. I don't want to lose you, especially not because you have some idiot notion you're an emotional cripple." His grip tightened, and he drew her to him so that he could hold her with both arms. "Believe me, Carol. Believe. Let me inside where you're warm and soft and giving. Let me show you how to love and give you love. Don't shut me out."

When he had her entirely in his embrace, his mouth covered hers at the last whispered word. And carefully he began to build the fires once again, and she melted against him and sought the warmth of his love. He kissed her long and gently. Then she slept, as peacefully as a child.

The sun was making the room bright and welcoming when Carol opened her eyes again. She had barely begun to recognize where she was when a sound at the door caught her attention. Zach shouldered the door open and stepped inside, a tray holding two coffee mugs and a coffeepot in his hands.

"How about some coffee?"

Carol sat up, drawing the sheet with her. Tucking it beneath her arms, she reached for the steaming cup of fragrant liquid he offered. Zach poured his own, then met her gaze across the rim of his cup as he sipped at it.

"How do you feel this morning?"

"A little off balance." Her blue gaze met his. "But, then, I've felt that way most of the time since meeting you."

"That's good. Never works to let a woman become too sure of you," he teased, lightening the tension between them.

"It's not a position I...enjoy. I like knowing where I stand."

"You're not alone in that. But, the question you're asking is where do you stand with me." At her tentative nod, his hand cupped her face in a gentle gesture of understanding. "I think that's up to you."

Drawing a deep breath, Carol forced her gaze to meet his directly. "I have a lot of fence-mending to do before I can go on with my life. I've started. I really have. But there's a long way to go." She slid to the edge of the bed. "And I'm starting today."

His gaze made adrenaline spurt through her. "Care to postpone that for a while?" His hand trailed down her arm to catch her hand.

Uncertainly she stood, the sheet still wrapped about her, looking down at him. "Zach, last night...I shouldn't have stayed...."

"Hey," he said, "nothing happened. I held you. Kept all the dragons at bay." He grinned. "And wished I could have done a hell of a lot more."

"Don't you ever have doubts, uncertainties?" Her gaze met his unwaveringly.

"I sure as hell do, and you're the biggest of them. But I know what I want."

"And that is?"

"You. I want you, from now on, until we grow gray and feeble together. I want to appreciate your strengths and help support you when you're afraid and have the lonelies. I want to hold you and love you and know you as well as I know myself. And I want the same from you."

"You're asking a lot."

"I plan on giving a lot."

"I don't know about those things...love, security." She hitched the sheet higher across her breasts and flushed warmly when his gaze followed the line of the sheet hem.

"Then let me teach you." He tugged on her hand and drew her down into his lap. Stiffly, she let him hold her. "Relax. Loving doesn't always mean going to bed. I just want to hold you a few minutes."

Capitulating suddenly, Carol relaxed. Her head rolled against his shoulder, and she let her eyes flutter closed. She reveled in the feel of his arms about her, in the warmth and encouragement of his embrace. And a little bud of trust began to blossom inside her.

The afternoon was nearly gone and Carol was looking forward to seeing the day end when the telephone on her desk buzzed. Still concentrating on the folders open before her, she reached absently for the receiver.

"Yes?"

"How about dinner tonight?"

"Zach! I didn't think I'd hear from you today."

"Thought you'd gotten rid of me? Not on your life, lady. I'm here for the duration."

"Duration?" A smile curved her lips. This man could touch her in so many ways it was frightening.

"Until you've made up your mind about us."

Her heart stopped in her chest and she swallowed dryly. "Us?"

"Don't pretend you don't know what I'm talking about. I thought I'd made it abundantly clear this morning where I want our relationship to go. You're the only thing holding up progress."

Carol flushed, memory curving her lips into a gentle smile. There was no doubt that Zach Taylor had the key to the passionate part of her personality. She became liquid in his hands, and she loved touching him and being touched.

Zach's husky voice was seductive, rolling across the telephone. "Are you remembering? Thinking about what almost happened?"

"You...ah...Zach, where are you?" She cleared her throat, but the tightness was still there.

His chuckle came over the wire. "In my office, and my secretary is here along with the chairman of the Taylor board of directors, and I'd like to have you here on the rug, beneath me...."

"Zachary!" Carol sat upright in the chair.

This time his hearty laugh greeted her indignation. "Do you think I'd share you with anyone? Everyone is gone. I'm here in the office alone, and I'd still like to have you here with me, but I'll settle for dinner in some public place. I have a surprise for you."

"A surprise? What?"

"It wouldn't be a surprise if I told you. I'll pick you up in half an hour. Can you be finished by then?"

"Sure, I'm about ready to quit now. I'll meet you downstairs."

"Good."

After he'd hung up, Carol slowly replaced the receiver. She was smiling, and when she realized it, she was almost startled. For the first time in a long while she felt completely relaxed. She had always been driven to achieve, to prove something to herself or to someone else, but now she was just looking forward to spending a quiet evening with the man...the man she loved.

The thought popped into her head without warning. She leaned back in her chair and toyed with it for a moment. Love. What a nice word. She tested it, rolling it over on her tongue and planting it in her mind. I love Zachary Taylor.

Thirty minutes had passed before she jerked her mind back to the present. Closing files and putting them in a top drawer before locking her desk, her fingers fumbled in anticipation. In just a few minutes she would be seeing Zach...her man. Her Cajun man. And she was smiling when she entered the downstairs foyer to find him waiting.

They had ordered dinner and were relaxing over a glass of wine before Carol's curiosity got the better of her.

"What kind of surprise do you have for me?"

"Well, now that I think of it, I'm not too certain of it. Something else might be better, but I'm not sure you're ready for it."

"Now I am intrigued. What are you talking about?"

"I'll show you later. First, I want to sit here and enjoy sharing a meal with you." He reached for her hand across the table. "It's what I like doing with you second best."

His teasing always made her body flush, and it did so now. "You're such an open man, Zach. I wish I could be more like you in that way."

"I like discovering that under the right circumstances, the aggressive and dynamic J. C. Martin can blush like a schoolgirl. It reveals the depth of complexity in you. I'll never be bored as long as you're with me."

Her blue eyes lifted to meet his gaze. "And how long do you think that will be?"

"I told you. Forever."

She studied his serious face at length. "That scares me to death."

"I know. But I want a long-term commitment."

"How...long term?" she whispered, seeking confirmation.

"I'm thinking in terms of marriage, of forever, Joan Carol. I don't put time limits on this kind of thing."

"I have a lot of thinking to do before I can begin to consider any kind of commitment."

"I know. And I'll wait as long as I can. But I warn you, last night only whetted my appetite for you. It will be awfully lonely in that bed until you can see fit to end my misery."

Again Carol studied him, judging the depth of his sincerity. "You really mean that, don't you?"

"I never meant anything more."

The New Orleans night was balmy when they strolled from the restaurant later. Her hand was linked with his, and Carol felt marvelously light and airy. It was a heady experience, finding a new depth to one's sensuality—a sensuality she had been convinced she didn't have. She was learning that just being with Zach was exciting. When other women looked at him, she felt jealousy—another newly discovered emotion. She looked forward to seeing him, to hearing his voice on the phone. She hungered for the physical expression of love. This was a Joan Carol DuBois she hardly recognized.

In the car, Zach drove from the French Quarter via Rampart Street. She thought at first he was returning to his home, but when he took the Pontchartrain Expressway she glanced at him questioningly.

"Where are we going?"

"To see my surprise."

Deciding he was determined to enjoy his little secret, Carol relaxed and enjoyed the drive across the Mississippi River onto the West Bank Expressway.

Zach exited the expressway onto a residential street, and soon they were entering a suburban area that Carol remembered was called Gretna. It was in the south side of the city. In a few minutes he drew the car to a halt before a block of new condominiums.

"What is this?" Carol asked as Zach turned in the car seat toward her.

"Your surprise." It seemed there was more uncertainty in the dark gaze holding hers. "I know you aren't ready for any commitments, but I hate your living in that hotel room. It seems so cold, so impersonal. I hate leaving you there every night." He released a long breath and flexed his shoulders restlessly. "So, I thought a place of your own... Look, if you don't like it, we can look at something else, but I thought you should at least see it...."

A smile began slowly and widened. "Oh, Zach." Her hand rested on his lean jaw. "No one has ever done anything like this for me before."

He relaxed visibly. "Come inside. I think you'll like it."

Carol watched as Zach quickly rounded the car and opened her door. Her heart was full. Even if she didn't like the condo, she would live there, because Zach had found it for her.

But she loved it. It was light and open, all wood and glass, and the colors were earth tones. Though it was empty of furniture, it held great promise.

"Zach, this is beautiful! I could never have found anything to match it. How did you hear about it?"

"A friend of mine moved out a few weeks ago and hadn't found a buyer. I called him this afternoon, and here we are. You'll need furniture, of course, unless you have some in Shreveport."

Carol looked around the living room again. The carpet was a dark blue, the walls were paneled in a light oak. The fireplace was natural stone, and the hearth was about six inches high—a perfect setting for lounging before the fire on the carpet and eating off the hearth. She conjured up pictures of herself and Zach there...this winter. She blinked. She was thinking awfully far ahead for a woman who had refused for years to be tied to anything permanent.

"I have some things stored, but I'll have to do some shopping."

When she would have gone into the bedroom for another look around, Zach pulled her about to face him. "This is only temporary, you know. As soon as you're ready, I want you in my home to make it *our* home. Think in those terms, all right?"

Her throat constricted in near panic. "I'll try, Zach. I'll really try."

His mouth closed over hers, and the gentle kiss turned into one of passion. "That's a promise I'll hold you to."

They took one more tour around the two-bedroom condo, making mental notes of things Carol wanted to buy, then returned to the car. Once inside, Carol inhaled deeply and looked once more at the house.

"I love it, Zach. I really love it."

"And does that extend to the man who found it for you?"

Carol turned and looked at him. "Yes, it does," she whispered. "It most certainly does."

"When you can say the words, then I'll know you're ready to trade this place for mine."

His fingers traced her lips. When her tongue slipped out to touch his fingertip, the subtle change in his face strummed her senses. It was exhilarating knowing she could excite this handsome man. Boldly her lips closed over the fingertip, and her teeth nibbled at it suggestively.

"Lord, woman. I want you. Now."

She smiled enigmatically. "And I want you."

"That's one step." And he gathered her into his arms and kissed her thoroughly—a promise of what was to come.

Chapter Ten

When Carol breezed into her office the next morning, there was a renewed sense of purpose about her.

"Anita, get DuBois on the line. I want to talk to my brother."

With an eyebrow raised in question the only indication of her doubt, Anita reached for the telephone. In a few moments she buzzed Carol.

"I'm sorry. John DuBois's secretary says he isn't in the office and won't be in all day."

Carol swiveled in her chair to look out the window, chewing a finger thoughtfully. "Sounds like big brother is really intent on avoiding me. I tried to reach him earlier at home, and they said he'd already left for the office." She thought for a moment. "All right, I guess that means I'll have to confront him in person. Thanks, Anita. I have several things to do this morning, then lunch with Zach Taylor, and then I'll deal with John, if I can find him."

"You're sure you want to do this?" Anita asked, knowing the whole story now.

"It's something I have to take care of before I can go forward. John has to understand why I handled things as I did."

"Okay. If there's anything I can do..."

"Thanks, Anita. Unless Zach calls, I'm unavailable this morning."

With that, Carol swiveled back to her desk, replaced the telephone receiver and forced her concentration on the folders in front of her. Two hours, a stack of folders and several telephone calls later, a smile of satisfaction curved Carol's mouth. Well, brother John, she said to herself, you'll have to acknowledge me now.

The intercom interrupted her moment of reverie. "Yes?"

"Your lunch date is here." A note of laughter in Anita's voice signified Zach had turned on the charm.

"Well, tell him to get off your desk and leave the help alone. I'll be right out."

The smile lingered and joy welled up inside her. For the first time in a long while she felt comfortable with herself. The driven quality was gone. Oh, she was still ambitious, still filled with a need to be her own person and the best in her profession, but there was an added dimension to her life now that softened the edges. And she liked the feeling it gave her. She liked knowing that Zach Taylor loved her just as she was, foibles and failings and all.

Stepping from her office, Carol's smile widened. Zach was dressed in a three-piece business suit of charcoal gray that complemented the smoky black of his hair and eyes. Strangely she felt shy and unnerved by her strong reactions to him.

"Hi." The word stuck in her throat. She caught Anita's eyebrow-lifted look of surprise and her unnatural quietness.

"Hi, yourself. Let's go." He winked at Anita. "I wouldn't want to keep your boss past her lunch hour."

"I'll be back by two, Anita."

And with that, her whole concentration was on the man at her side.

"Did you have a good morning?" He looked down at her fondly.

A faint blush touched her cheeks. "Yes. I got quite a lot accomplished. Didn't reach John, though. He's still avoiding me. I'm thinking of confronting him directly."

Zach opened the car door for her, leaning over as she slid inside. "Is that really what you want to do? It could be uncomfortable."

"It's something that has to be done. He needs to understand why I did those things, and I need a better situation between us."

"It isn't necessary for us," he assured her, and his dark eyes substantiated his statement.

Reaching up, she rested a hand against his lean cheek. "I know. But it's necessary for me. I've carried around a lot of bitterness and I have to get rid of it before I can . . . consider a commitment to you."

"'Consider'? I thought we'd talked through all that. I want you as you are."

"But you're still willing to wait until I feel able to enter into a fully committed relationship with you . . . ?"

"The word marriage scares you that much? You can't even say the word?"

"The idea scares me. Everything it means. In spite of anything I tell myself, I'm still afraid. Before I come to you, I want everything cleared up—the guilt about my marriage, the situation between myself and John. Her thumb traced his lips. "Please say you understand, that you'll let me do this my way."

"I don't understand, honey, but I can accept that you need to do this. I'd marry you this afternoon if you'd just say the word. But I can wait if you feel you have to do this first."

"Thank you, Zach. I don't know what good fairy sent you my way, but I hope she's here to stay."

And with a quick kiss planted across her lips, Zach closed the door and rounded the car to slide into the driver's seat. When he hesitated before starting the car, Carol turned to him questioningly.

"You know, I guess I do have to admit that something good came from your scheming," he said.

"Oh? And what's that?"

"We'd have never met again otherwise. You'd have been in Shreveport or wherever and John would never have had reason to call me if his business hadn't been in trouble." He leaned toward her in the small confines of the car. His breath brushed her cheek, and his dark eyes bored into her. "Good does sometimes come out of trouble." And this time when he kissed her, it was no fleeting thing. His mouth slanted on hers, and his hand at the back of her head reinforced the hardness of his kiss. She opened to him, her whole body responding to his lovemaking, seeking the reassurance that Zach meant everything he said—that he loved her, loved every part of her.

Reluctantly Zach released her. "If we're going to get any lunch—without ordering room service—I think I'd better drive. Passersby are beginning to look at us."

"Let them look. They're just jealous." Her voice was husky with desire.

"Don't look at me like that, lady, or we will end up back at the hotel, and I think the desk man is beginning to suspect something already."

"When will my condo be ready?" she asked suggestively.

"I spoke to my friend this morning. Everything is arranged. All you need is furniture."

"And I spoke to someone in Shreveport who can ship what I left. I should have some stuff arriving early next week. By that time maybe I can pick up some of the other things I need."

"Don't pick anything you don't want in *our* house. I'm hoping it won't be long before we can plan a little merger of our own."

Carol's hand rested on his thigh, and she could feel Zach's muscles flex beneath her sensitive fingers. Her body warmed in the thought of other muscles flexing beneath caressing fingers in a much more intimate place. "Just keep believing in me, Zach. I need that."

"I believe in you. But I'm not immune to being hurt, Carol. If I didn't believe you're worth the risk, I wouldn't be taking it. No one looks for that kind of heartache."

Suddenly the light atmosphere was heavy with unspoken words. "I don't want to hurt you, Zach. I'd rather lose you now than risk ..."

Zach swerved the car from the line of traffic and pulled into a loading zone. She blinked in surprise when he left the motor idling and turned to her in the seat. "You're not about to lose me, lady. You're coming to me, on your own terms right now. But if you take too long, then it will be on my terms."

"And what are those terms?" Her voice was a whisper as she studied his grim face.

"I can step into this thing with John and the Du-Bois company. I can speak to him, make him understand, or I can drop a few words in the right places that could make him listen to you."

"You wouldn't interfere." She hadn't considered that he might do exactly as he threatened and that he could do it. She'd been thinking of herself and John only in business terms and of herself and Zach only in personal terms. But Zach had the power, the influence, to do exactly what he said.

"I could, and I will if you take too long to do it on your own."

"But I have to do it my way...."

"You've done everything to this point your way. You're accustomed to having your way... in business and in your personal life. When your marriage died, it seems you determined to never let anyone have influence over you again. I saw that the first time we met, before I knew who you were. You directed the conversation at the charity ball, started it when you chose and left when you chose. And you manipulated John's business, and I understand your reasons for that. But when it comes to you and me and our personal lives, decisions have to be mutual. We're part of each other—one of us isn't in the power seat."

"I wouldn't try..."

"You're doing it now. Making us wait until you're sure all the loose ends are tied up. It would be just as simple to get married now and talk to John later. But you have to do it your way. I understand, but I'm saying, don't think you can continue to live a solitary existence once we're married. We will continue to be individuals, certainly, but we have to be 'together' on everything. Times like this I wonder if you can understand or accept that.''

Startled by the vehemence in his voice and attitude, Carol sat looking at Zach. ''I didn't realize ... I'm sorry.'' Closing her eyes for a moment to cling to her composure, Carol accepted what he said. ''I'm so accustomed to thinking for myself and to making decisions for others that I do it automatically. I still have to learn that loving includes trusting someone and not taking them for granted. I'm trying. Be patient with me?''

A smile lightened his countenance. ''That's something I never thought I would hear J. C. Martin say.''

She laughed, relieved. ''What did you think J. C. Martin would say?''

''In light of the fact that I thought this mysterious character was some burly backwater Louisianian, some shyster out to undercut a competitor, I figured threats would be more in 'his' line. You can imagine how I felt when I discovered 'he' was a petite girl with nerves of steel, but a heart just waiting to melt like a marshmallow.''

With her head cocked to one side and a smile playing about her lips, Carol couldn't resist teasing him. '''Marshmallow'? We hard-core business types resent being compared to marshmallows. You wouldn't say that if you'd been a mouse in the corner of my office this morning. I consummated some deals that would make your head spin.''

"Consummated. I like that word. How about meeting at my place to discuss the possibilities of that word being a permanent part of our vocabulary?" he asked, breathing the words seductively against her lips.

"Mmm, I like the idea. But if we don't move on, we're going to get towed away, and I don't think the city auto park is where we want to be when we have that kind of discussion."

Smiling, he relented. "Hard-core, definitely hard-core. Here I was just warming up... but later I won't be so easily put off."

"I'm counting on it." And she kissed him again before he engaged the gears and reentered the traffic flow.

Chapter Eleven

A couple of weeks passed and Carol was extremely busy. She and Zach spent their time together making plans for her move into the condo. Her boxes and furniture arrived from Shreveport, and Zach and Carol spent one weekend choosing odd pieces of furniture to place temporarily in her new home. She noticed that whenever she began to sound too permanent in her plans for the house, Zach brought up some decorating question about his own house, reminding her that he hoped one day she would be moving into it as Mrs. Zachary Taylor.

On Thursday of the second week her intercom buzzed. Marking her place in the margin of a report she was reading, Carol absently reached for the phone.

"Yes?"

"What are you up to, Joan Carol?"

"Zach? What's the matter?"

"I just spoke to John. He's got an unbelievable up-surge in accounts coming his way. They're phoning him, instead of him calling them. What are you doing?"

Carol settled back in her chair. "What makes you think I have anything to do with this happy circumstance?"

"It smacks of your manipulations. What are you doing? Trying to destroy every shred of his confidence?"

Carol straightened. "What are you talking about?"

"How would you feel if I started feeding you accounts, talking to people, strongly suggesting I would be pleased if they shunted work your direction?"

"Angry, I suppose. But that's not what I was doing."

"No? Haven't you contacted certain individuals who you knew were considering your company for computer installations and suggested they consider DuBois? I just wonder what you used as a reason."

His anger translated to her. "I didn't need a reason. CCC is moving in another direction. When anyone came to us for a bid, I simply suggested they consider DuBois. The rest is John's doing. If he's so insecure as to think I would send jobs to him out of charity or without believing DuBois could handle them, then he's even less a businessman than I gave him credit for. And I do give him some credit."

The silence at the other end of the line made her grip tighten on the receiver. "Then you didn't exactly pull any strings?"

"No. I decided I couldn't honestly be in competition with my own brother. Whether you believe it or not, I felt guilty every time I took a bid away from him. At the time I thought it was a necessary move to make a point. But I don't make the same mistake twice."

"You were willing to crucify John to make a point a few weeks ago."

"I admit I went about things wrong, but I couldn't think of any other way to do it. I still can't. Given the same circumstances, I might do the same thing again."

"Oh? I'm not sure I like that."

Stiffening in her chair, Carol carefully considered her next words. "I'm not perfect, Zach. I won't ever be, not even with your careful tutelage. But with you, I have a sounding board, should such a circumstance ever occur again. Still, the choices I make will be my own."

"I see."

"I don't think you do. I think you expected me to follow meekly along under your direction. You accuse me of manipulating, and yet you do the same thing. You've made a few mistakes, I'll bet, so don't act like some all-knowing god when it comes to mine." Her words were clipped.

"I think enough has been said on the subject. See you later."

Without responding, Carol replaced the receiver in its cradle. A headache was blossoming at the base of her skull. Tension. All she needed now was a rip-roaring tension headache. Opening her purse, Carol tipped two tablets into her palm and poured a glass of water from the carafe on the corner of her desk. Swallowing the aspirin, she sat with her eyes closed for a few moments, willing the ache to subside. When it didn't, she determined to forget the conversation with Zach and concentrated on her work. Just getting

through the afternoon now would be difficult enough
without dwelling on the accusation in Zach's voice.

At six Carol finally gave up pretending to work.
Zach hadn't called back, and she felt certain he would
not be coming by as had become his practice. She went
back to spend her last night alone in the hotel room.

Her key slid into the lock easily. After all, she
thought, I've opened this door hundreds of times since
coming to New Orleans. The hotel room felt cold and
looked dismal. The tasteful decor taunted her with its
perfect combination of bland color and fabric. The
impersonal perfection of cleanliness mocked her. At
one time she would have welcomed the sterile feel of
the room. But now she longed for something
more...more welcoming.

Suddenly she spun on her heel and exited the room.
Back outside, she slid into her car and in a few minutes was headed toward the condominium that would
be her home for a little while. Possibly longer than
she'd originally thought, if Zach could not understand her way of dealing with the conflict between
herself and John.

The condo sat dark and waiting. After unlocking
the door, Carol stepped inside and flipped on a light.
The furniture had arrived and had been placed in a
haphazard manner. And although she was still dressed
in her office clothes, Carol bent to the task of arrang-
ing it in a more acceptable manner.

Kicking off her shoes and tossing aside the jacket of
her suit, Carol rolled up the sleeves of her tailored
lemon-colored silk blouse. The style of her white linen
straight skirt did not lend itself well to the kind of
movement necessary to shove about chairs and sofas,
so after a few minutes she slipped off the skirt, too.

In an hour she had the living room arranged to her satisfaction and began working on the kitchen. After being given a quick washing, the dishes were soon placed in the cabinet, and Carol was beginning to feel the place was really her own.

A sound at the front door brought her attempt to place rarely used dishes on the top shelf of the cabinet to a halt. Perched on the countertop on her knees, Carol waited. A tingle of apprehension that she would admit as fear moved up her spine.

"Carol?" Zach called out. In but a moment he stood in the kitchen door. "What are you doing up there, and dressed like that? You can't believe what I thought when I saw pieces of your clothing scattered about the living room."

Sinking onto her haunches, Carol faced him, with disgust marking her smudged and flushed face. "You scared me to death, Zachary Taylor. What are you doing here?"

Zach stepped across the room to lift her down from the cabinet. He purposely let his hands linger at her waist as he slid her down his hard body. "I couldn't stay angry with you. I wanted to talk, but the hotel clerk said you'd left again shortly after coming in from the office. I took a chance you would be here."

Ignoring the suggestion in his body language, Carol stepped aside, suddenly aware of her half-dressed state. "Excuse me. I think I'd better make myself more presentable."

"Don't do it on my account. I like you just the way you are."

Sensing a double meaning in his words, Carol glanced up at Zach. "That wasn't what I heard this afternoon," she reminded him.

His hand at her waist stopped her escape attempt. "I admit I was angry, and I probably jumped to conclusions. You're a difficult woman to understand, and I sometimes find myself falling into old traps."

"Old traps?"

"Yeah." His fingers combed through his already tousled hair. "Physical desire, need. A need to hold you and protect you, to have you need me. But I realize you don't always want those things."

"I always need those things. Sometimes I just don't accept them. I could easily become too dependent on you, Zach. And it's a feeling I'm finding difficult to come to terms with. I need you." Her hand rested at the side of his neck, her fingers teasing the crisp curls resting on his nape, her thumb lying in the hollow of his cheek. "And sometimes that scares me. I have to remain my own person. Just as you said, we are what we must be at our respective offices, but when we're together, we must be...together. If we disagree about business, let it be just that. Business. Let's not carry it into our private lives."

"Can we do that?"

"If it's what we both want, we can. Is it what you want?"

Zach gathered her close, pressing her body against his, burrowing his face into the curve of her neck. He breathed deeply of her special fragrance. "You know it is. I guess I just lost sight of what the future can mean for us if we both work at it."

Hungrily her arms lifted and curved about his shoulders. The feel of him excited her. He had changed from his business suit to more casual corduroys and a knit shirt that molded to him. She could feel the warmth of him through the fabric. The softness of his shirt caressed her cheek when she rested her face against his chest. His heart beat strongly, matching the cadence of her own accelerated pulse.

"I want that," she whispered. "I want everything with you. If I lost you now, I don't know what I would do."

His hand slid the silken fabric of her half slip upward, moving over the firm curve of her buttocks as he drew her ever closer to him. "I'm sorry," he whispered into her hair. "I'm sorry I jumped to conclusions and didn't take the time to talk about what you were doing to help DuBois."

She stiffened in his arms. "Why did you jump to those conclusions? If you love me, you should assume I'm doing the right thing."

When she would have pushed away from him, his hands gripped her upper arms. "Carol, don't do this. I'm trying to apologize."

"Apologize? You're the one always talking about how perfect our love can be, about trusting and believing in people. Yet you always think the worst of me. I don't think I can believe you." She pushed at him again, and his grip tightened. "Let me go, Zach. I want to get dressed."

"No. You listen to me. I'm not going to let you drive a wedge between us now."

"Me? I didn't do anything. I was just trying to help my brother, make him understand I didn't mean to ruin him personally. Yes, I wanted to prove something. I wanted to prove that he's out of his element and that I can help him. If he's feeling insecure, that's his problem. You, more than anyone else, should realize that confidence comes from within. Part of that is finding where you belong in the scheme of things.

You did it. I have. And John must. I decided to help him succeed so that he'd have the time to reevaluate and come to his own conclusions about what to do with his life."

"I thought John had already done that. He seems pretty content."

"Ever since Father died, John has been swamped with the business of learning about the company, of having to cope with the expansion Father started. John hasn't had time to really consider whether he's in the right place or not, or he's too stubborn to be honest with himself about it. I just want to give him time to think, really think."

This time, when she pushed against him, Zach let her go. Carol strode into the living room and picked up her skirt. Dressed, she would be better able to cope with Zach and his judgments.

Zach followed her into the room, watching as she stepped into the skirt and zipped it up. "I think I liked you the other way better."

Carol spun about accusingly, and the glint of humor in Zach's eyes only increased her anger.

"I thought you didn't want want to fall into the 'trap' of wanting a woman only on a physical level. Isn't that what happened in your marriage?" she said savagely, wanting to hurt him as he'd hurt her.

"Yes, it was." His dark eyes were pinning her to the spot.

Her skirt in place, Carol felt more comfortable. "Then?"

"Infatuation is such a superficial word. But that's all there was between my wife and me. When things got bad between us, we each closed ourselves off, and then she began to seek 'comfort' elsewhere." At her look, he continued quickly. "Oh, there was no affair as such, but there were long afternoons of unexplained absences when she could have easily been with another man. There was the opportunity. I credit her with not going that far. At least we recognized the trouble we were in and ended it amiably." He drew a deep breath and released it slowly. "At that, it was not a pleasant experience. I felt the same sense of failure you've described to me. I've spent nights wondering what I could have done differently, and I've reached out and found no one on the other side of a very wide and lonely bed. I'm tired of all that."

Carol drew herself up straight. "And that's where I come in?"

"Not exactly. I've already come to terms with my failures. I know what I want from a woman, from a marriage. I don't think you've come to that point. Not yet."

"You know me so well?"

"I'm learning."

In the face of his calmness, her frustration mounted. "I don't think you understand me at all." She picked up her suit jacket and slipped her arms into the sleeves. Jerking at the lapel to settle the garment across her shoulders, she glanced about the room to locate the purse she had tossed aside a few hours earlier.

"Looking for this?" He held her bag in his outstretched hand.

"Yes. I'm leaving." She reached for it, but Zach held the purse away from her.

"You're not leaving until we've finished talking."

"There's nothing more to discuss. You doubt my motives, and in spite of everything you say, our strongest area of compatibility lies in physical attraction. I don't think I like being reduced to a plaything."

Lifting her purse just out of reach again, Zach grinned down at her. "You are a thing of pleasure. And I like our being compatible that way. But there are other levels where we meet, and once you're over being angry with me, I think you'll recognize that." With his free hand he clasped the back of her neck to hold her still against him. "I came here to apologize, not to start another argument."

Something in his voice, something behind the smiling curve of his mouth, arrested the words that sprang to her lips. For a moment their gazes held, measuring, judging. Then Carol relaxed against Zach.

When his arms lowered to settle about her, she knew this was what she wanted. The purse, as a source of contention between them, was forgotten, and he tossed it aside to allow his hand to curve around her waist. The tension that had been heightening between them since his arrival shifted subtly from anger to assume a more sexual tone.

Zach's hands slid down Carol's back to mold her to his hard frame. His warm breath brushed her mouth before his kiss replaced it. Closing her eyes, she accepted his kiss, feeding the tiny flame of passion beginning to flicker between them. It was always the same. He touched her, and she became warm clay to be molded in his experienced hands.

"I'm sorry. I came here to apologize and to say I love you. I thought we might drink a little wine, hold each other a little. I just wanted to hold you, tell you I was wrong to accuse you rather than to listen to what you had to say."

"And I'm sorry I lashed out at you. I really am trying to help John."

"I know. Today, when I learned about the sharp upswing in bids going his way, I immediately suspected the worst. I told myself that if you really loved me, you would have told me what you were doing. And that made me angry."

"You're right. I should have told you first. But I'm not used to sharing with anyone—business or pleasure. But I set things in motion concerning DuBois some time ago. Before...before things went this far with us." Her fingers traced the outline of his strong firm mouth. "I have a lot to learn, Zach, about sharing, about being open and giving. I demand a lot of myself and others. I hope you know what you're doing when you take me on, Mr. Taylor. I sometimes fear for us both."

"We're a team, lady, though you're a little slow to acknowledge it."

For an answer, Carol went up on tiptoes and brushed a tantalizing kiss across his mouth. Taking the initiative, Zach crushed her to him and deepened the kiss, moving on her lips and exploring within until she was melting against him.

Taking Carol with him, Zach sank onto the couch and drew her across his chest as he sprawled across the cushions. She came willingly, fitting her smaller frame to his as his hands pressed her hips more firmly to his. She was fully aware of the strength of the passion that sparked so easily between them.

Slipping her fingers inside his shirt collar, Carol reveled in the feel of his warm skin before moving down to loosen the buttons of his shirt.

"I think it was foolish of you to put that skirt back on. It's only in the way," he teased, his voice husky.

Carol laughed, a bubble of happiness bursting inside her and making its way through her body. "I'm sure that's never been a problem for you."

"Mmmm, I like this new person you've become." His long fingers brushed through her hair, and his expression grew serious as he studied the contours of her face. "I appreciate the serious side of you, the part that is a businesswoman, but I enjoy being able to laugh with you."

"You've totally perverted me, you know." With the tip of her forefinger, Carol smoothed the thick arch of Zach's eyebrow. "I find my attention wandering at the most inopportune times. When I should be putting together a proposal, instead I'm imagining what you're doing, who you're with, and wonder if you're thinking of me."

When her words trailed off, Zach prodded her attention back to the subject. "Why the perplexed look? Isn't that the way people in love react? It's natural for there to be a certain amount of inattention to detail, a little indulging in daydreaming."

"Maybe that's natural for you, but it's totally out of character for me. I've always been a single-minded woman, and you've shaken up my priorities."

His hand stilled, dropping to rest on her shoulder. "Does that worry you?"

"Worry? No, but it does give me an unaccustomed sense of imbalance that I find difficult to deal with."

"Are you sorry we met, that we were attracted to each other?"

Carol studied Zach's serious countenance for a long moment, seeing the tension lurking in his dark eyes.

Slowly a smile curved her lips. "No. I may be a drudge, but I'm no fool. I know happiness when it bowls me over." Playfully she nipped his earlobe, drinking in the faint aroma of cologne, reveling in the freedom to react openly to the potent pull of his masculinity.

Zach folded her in his arms, holding her against him with a feeling of relief. The Carol he held was not the same woman who had deliberately encountered and baited him at the historical society dance. That woman had been a brittle shell, protecting the one who now lay so pliantly, so receptively in his arms. He much preferred the new Carol.

Nuzzling against him, planting small kisses against Zach's neck, Carol felt a chuckle begin to rumble deep in his chest. She looked down into his smiling eyes. "What are you laughing at?"

"You and me. We're sprawled over this couch, my feet hanging off the end and your hair hanging in your face. What clothes we have on are rumpled. You'd think we were a couple of teenagers trying to get in a little heavy petting before our folks come home. There's a perfectly good bed upstairs just waiting for us."

"Zach . . ." Carol began.

His dark eyes darkened even more. "Come, be my lady tonight."

She wanted to. There was nothing on earth she wanted more. He could just look at her and she was ready to follow him anywhere. But it had to be the right time, the right place. She'd made so many mistakes. This time . . . it had to be right.

His gaze held her. It seemed as if he were reading her mind. For a long moment his head rested against the couch. Obeying a sudden urge to commune with him, to share and touch, her fingers brushed his crisp hair back and forth in a hypnotic movement.

She was still amazed at the changes this man in her arms had made in her life. Only a few months earlier, if someone had suggested that she would let down her carefully constructed armor and allow anyone to see her at her most vulnerable, she would have considered that person utterly crazy. She would have considered a suggestion that she might fall in love with someone like Zach even crazier. For although he was strong and determined in his own way, Zach was still a man who took things in stride, changing his course on a whim, choosing to enjoy life rather than dictate its outcome—a complete contrast to her structured way of living.

The realization of how Zach had affected her life was frightening, but not frightening enough, she admitted, to make her turn from him. In acknowledging that weakness, which she was beginning to recognize as a new form of strength, she knew the ability to love was growing inside her.

"Have I told you what a difference you've made in my life?"

Zach's chuckle rumbled in his chest, vibrating against her sensitive skin. "Sounds like a song title."

Curling a wisp of his hair about her forefinger, Carol tugged lightly. "Surrender, you cad. No fair of you to mock my pitiful attempt to express how I feel." A smile accompanied the teasing rebuke. "You've turned my world upside down."

"Lady, if we're comparing upheavals, it's a toss-up. I never thought I'd consider settling down with a tiny blond, blue-eyed iron butterfly, even if she was just emerging from her cocoon.''

Her smile widened. "I dare you to repeat that.''

"Can't. Besides, actions speak louder than words. You know us Cajuns. Always take the easiest trail, never do today what can be done tomorrow, especially if it's work, and always take pleasure above duty—though you've played havoc with my 'pleasure' lately." He turned and pulled her against him, his smile fading to seriousness. His fingers threaded through her tangled hair. "I love you, Joan Carol.''

When his mouth covered hers in a demanding kiss, she relaxed against him, her fingers spreading across his chest in a caressing possessiveness.

"I love you, Zachary Taylor." She returned his kisses willingly. It was much later before Zach took her back to the hotel.

Chapter Twelve

Anita..." Carol began as she strode into her offices.

"I know, call John. Carol, this isn't going to work." She was dialing the now familiar DuBois number as she spoke.

"Try once more. If he won't talk to me this time, clear my calendar for late this afternoon. It's time this was settled. I'll go over there, exert my prerogative as a DuBois and stay until my brother listens to me."

"I don't know, J. C. You're sure you want to pursue this? His ego has taken a terrible beating with you practically sabotaging the company, then resurrecting it. He may think you're toying with him again."

"Then I'll just have to convince him otherwise. I'll have some dictation in about twenty minutes."

Carol strode decisively into her office and poured a cup of coffee from the carafe Anita always made certain was on her desk each morning.

Once again her secretary was unable to reach John DuBois. Carol would have to find another way to reach her brother. She began to plan just how to accomplish that.

The day passed quickly. CCC was progressing well without the burden of assuming the projects she had taken on to undercut John, and she felt good about the figures on the balance sheet that lay before her on the desk. In a short time she'd turned a fast-failing business around and planted it firmly among its competitors as a company to be considered seriously. She could well be proud of that accomplishment. And she was. It was the more personal side of her decision to go into business for herself that gave her life the cloud that continued to shadow her happiness.

Another troublesome thought crossed her mind. What about CCC if she accepted Zach's proposal of marriage? As a Southern gentleman of the old school and as a product of the Cajun heritage of which he was so very proud, would he expect her to follow in the line of his female ancestors and concern herself with the many charities that held his interest? Somehow she couldn't envision herself fitting into that role.

A small frown creased her forehead. If she seriously considered marriage with Zach, would she be falling once again into the same smothering trap she'd escaped by divorcing Alex Martin? He'd been so jealous of her accomplishments, belittling her as a woman so often that she'd sought sanctuary in the work he'd ridicule until she couldn't stand the strain any longer. She couldn't let that happen again.

At five-thirty Anita peeked around Carol's office door. "I'm leaving, unless there's something else."

Startled by the swift passage of time, Carol glanced at her watch. "No, nothing, Anita. Thanks."

"Ah, I still haven't reached your brother."

"I know. I guess I'll stop by the house."

"You haven't been to the house since you left for college, have you?" Anita asked.

"No, and I'm overdue, don't you think?" Carol stood and straightened the files that had lain on her desk open but unread all afternoon. "I'll see you in the morning, Anita."

Carol stood looking out over the traffic-clogged streets, reliving the last confrontation with her father, then moved on to the last meeting with her brother when he'd learned how deeply her resentments had cut. Disappointment—in herself, in the way she'd handled her pain—reopened the unhealed wounds. She'd made a lot of mistakes, big mistakes, but now was the time to try to correct some of them.

With determination firming her lips, Carol picked up the phone and dialed a number from memory. When a man's voice answered, the grim look on her face softened.

"Can I see you later tonight? I may need a little of that Cajun charm."

Zach's response was immediate. "What are you doing?"

"I'm going out to the house to see John. This time I won't let him evade me or throw me out."

"Do you want me to go with you?" Zach sat at his desk, his jacket off, his shirt sleeves rolled to the elbow. It had been a long day, and he'd looked forward to being with Carol this evening.

"No, I started this on my own, so I have to finish it on my own."

Recognizing her need to mend fences, Zach capitulated. "I'll be at the house. Come home to me, Carol, when you're ready."

Carol gripped the receiver, suddenly needing to know the answer to a question that had plagued her. "Will you, Zach? And what will you expect of me if I come to you?"

He answered slowly. "I think that is something we have to discuss. But not tonight."

"Why not?"

"Because tonight I want to pamper and hold you. Solving one major problem per day is enough."

"Then you admit the question does pose a problem?"

"No, only that you tend to consider every unanswered question a problem."

Carol hesitated, biting back the retort that sprang to her lips. "Do I?"

Zach's chuckle came over the wire. "Honey, when are you ever going to learn to trust me? We'll talk tonight, when you come home."

Obstinacy reared its ugly head. She refused to be dictated to or taken for granted. "Maybe I won't come. I got myself into this mess. I can handle it all on my own."

"Carol—" a note of impatience was evident in his voice "—I'm not trying to tell you what to do. I'm just saying I'll be here when you need me."

Tears stung her eyes, and Carol blinked them back. "I don't know how to need anyone, Zach." The words were whispered.

"Carol, are you there? Carol . . ."

The voice faded away before Carol set the receiver down to break the connection. She didn't need anyone. Her body responded to Zach, and for a while she'd been thrown off balance by the enormity of what she'd almost done to her brother, but now that didn't matter. She'd proved her business ability, disproved Alex's accusation that she was incapable of responding to a man, and now she would prove to herself and to John that she could admit her mistakes and go on with her life. She just hoped John would understand and forgive her for nearly ruining him.

A short time later she'd claimed her car from the parking garage and was headed toward the section of New Orleans that had been her home until she was eighteen.

Nostalgia tugged at Carol as she drove through familiar streets. Too soon she was pulling into the driveway of a fashionable single-story structure that her father had built only two years before his wife died. As she turned off the ignition, Carol pushed aside the memories and slid from the car. She strode purposefully up the walk and pushed the doorbell with one manicured finger.

Footsteps signaled the approach of someone, and Carol stiffened her resolve. But when the door opened, a uniformed maid greeted Carol.

"I'd like to see John DuBois, please."

"May I say who is callin'?" came the drawled reply.

Carol's glance flicked past the young woman. "His sister, Carol."

Surprise widened the woman's eyes. "Why..."

With a sudden decisive movement, Carol pushed the door open wider and stepped into the foyer. It had changed little since her teen years. "Just tell John I'm here and I'm not leaving until he talks with me."

"Yes, ma'am." The light click of heels faded away toward the back of the house.

Carol stood at the window looking out into the yard. Memories flooded her once again. On more than one occasion the drive had been filled with cars of various vintages and states of disrepair. They'd held parties on the patio—cokes, burgers and hot dogs and, later, beer and pizza. Carol had been bouncy and bubbly; John, the quiet scholar, basking in the glow of her popularity. There had been only the cloud of their mother's early death on their sunny day of youth.

Carol sighed deeply, allowing her long fingers to knead the knot of tension at the base of her neck. She caught her reflection in a mirror over the mantel in the formal living room in which she'd taken her stand. Her eyes were wide in a pale face. Her lips were thin with determination and tension. That morning she'd pulled her hair into a chignon at the nape of her neck and secured it with pins, outlining her face with severity. She longed now to let it down and run her fingers through it to massage her scalp. Her feet hurt. Her shoulders ached. And she was afraid.

A sound at the door drew her attention. Her brother stood in the doorway, and he was angry.

Chapter Thirteen

"What do you want, Carol?" He remained standing in the doorway. He still wore a business suit, but his tie was loose. Carol imagined he'd arrived home not long before her.

"A chance to explain something to you. I think you owe me that much."

"I owe you nothing. You almost ruined me. There's nothing left to discuss."

"It wasn't exactly that way, John. Please, let's talk. Let's call a truce for just a short while. Give me that." He was unmovable. "This didn't begin six months ago, John, or even when Father died or when I decided to go to college for a business degree over Father's wishes. It all started...even before Mother's death."

"What are you talking about?" John shoved his hands into his trouser pockets.

"Didn't you notice? Weren't you aware that I was a kind of second-class citizen, especially after Mother died? It was as if I was born to be Father's personal whipping boy. And until I left for college, I accepted his dictate that I was useful only to hostess his few business dinners and function as housekeeper."

"I don't remember that. You're exaggerating his concern for you to..."

"'Concern'? John, you came and went as you pleased. Fortunately you weren't particularly interested in straining the boundaries of his autocratic rule, but, of course, you were the son. The inheritor. Any hell-raising you did would have been welcomed. I, on the other hand, was kept strictly under his thumb. Nothing I did was right!" Her voice had risen, and Carol gestured widely to emphasize her statement as her resentment and the residue of her frustration spewed forth.

John advanced into the room. "So you've made yourself the martyr in this? You alone suffered from his demanding nature? Let me enlighten you, dear sister. Let me tell you how life was under the 'guidance' of a man who second-guessed every decision he reluctantly allowed me to make, who when I joined the firm, finished every sentence I started, who insisted on changing, just a little, every proposal I created until the day he died!"

John advanced farther into the room until he stood before Carol. "You blame him for the shell you built around yourself? At least he allowed you to escape! I never had a prayer of living my own life, not even when I accepted the responsibility of the firm. Nothing was ever good enough. I wasn't aggressive enough or hard enough. To point out my deficiencies, on a few occasions, he'd even throw up your decisiveness, your refusal to bend to him.

"It wasn't easy, Carol. Not by a long shot. But I survived. Then you arrived on the scene."

When John stifled the explosion of words there was a long heavy silence. It was as if the whole house waited expectantly.

Carol drew a calming breath, her gaze never leaving John's fevered face. "You've changed the house very little."

John was slow to respond. "I suppose it just never seemed worth the effort."

"Why don't you move? Have a place of your own?"

"I don't know." His gaze moved around the room. "Even though he's dead..." There was no need to finish the sentence.

Again the waiting silence. Finally John drew a long breath and released it slowly. Carol waited, her nerves so tight that they quivered beneath her skin.

"I guess we do have a few things to talk about."

Together they sank onto the couch, and for the next two hours they exposed the inner secrets that had dictated the roads they'd traveled, the decisions they'd made in their lives.

Dark fell, dinner was forgotten and when the maid came to offer refreshments, she was waved absently away. Their total concentration was on each other.

Much later, as Carol drove back toward New Orleans proper, she felt drained. Her eyes were puffy from the tears of remorse she'd shed and her throat ached from holding back more. She felt as if she could sleep for years.

Without thinking, she drove to the office, seeking the comfort of the familiar. The condo was still too new, and she couldn't go to Zach. Not until she had sorted through everything she'd learned tonight.

The building was silent. The cleaning people had not yet come in. The solitude was salve to her lacerated emotions.

In the offices of CCC, Carol left off the lights, switching on only a small lamp in her own office. Swishing the remaining coffee in the carafe on her desk, she poured out a cool cup, grimacing at its tepid bitterness.

Kicking off her shoes, she flexed her cramped toes and stretched out on the couch until the back of her head rested against the cushions. Closing her eyes, Carol let the tears seep out until they made a stream down her pale cheeks. A small sob escaped, opening the door to allow the audible breaking of her heart to echo in the otherwise silent room.

She wasn't certain how much time had elapsed before the opening of the outer door caught her attention. The cleaning people, she thought, reluctantly forcing her mind and body to function. Her watch showed almost ten o'clock. She should go home, but somehow the sterile atmosphere of a hotel room seemed more inviting than the comfortable home she'd been crazy enough to begin putting together in the condo Zach had arranged for her to have.

Her office door pushed open before she had forced herself from the couch.

"Ready to go home?"

Startled, her head jerked toward the low masculine voice. "Zach! What are you doing here?"

"That's my line. I thought we'd reached an agreement."

"I think it was an impasse."

"Only on your part. I'm ready for the next step. You're the one dragging your feet."

By now he stood before her, and she felt at a definite disadvantage. Pushing to her feet, Carol brushed at her rumpled suit, avoiding his intense searching gaze.

But Zach was persistent. Lightly gripping her chin, he forced her face up to his. "Was it that bad?"

His sympathy and the understanding she saw mirrored in his dark eyes when she finally met them were her undoing. Her face crumpled and fresh tears glistened.

"Oh, Zach, I was so wrong. I thought I was the only one who suffered, but when I escaped, John kept paying and paying. I never realized how stubborn and autocratic and...and incapable of understanding or changing my father was. He was a tyrant, and I wasn't alone in my resentment of him."

"I take it you and John worked things out."

"Not entirely. But we're trying, and we have a new understanding of each other."

Zach picked up her shoes with two fingers and slipped an arm about her shoulders. "Let's go home and you can tell me about it."

Carol halted. "I can't talk about it yet."

A sad smile moved his lips. "Then I can wait."

"Can you understand why...why I can't talk about it?"

"Carol, when are you going to stop testing me, testing every emotional response?"

Her shoulders sagged. "I don't know." She felt like a petulant child. "I have a headache."

"Then I have an aspirin and a back rub."

Questioningly she glanced up at him. Reading the question, he responded. "Your every need I want to supply. Your every desire I want to fulfill."

White teeth nibbled at her lower lip. "I wish I could believe that."

"You can, if you'll just let yourself. Let someone else into your life—me. Only me."

His mouth brushed hers softly in promise, but she couldn't bring herself to respond. She was simply too emotionally and physically exhausted.

"Come on, sweet lady. Come with me. For once let me just take care of you."

She could do nothing else. She was incapable of even thinking beyond the moment, much less of working at keeping a wall erected between them.

Zach locked the doors of CCC behind them, and in a few minutes they were on the street, heading toward Zach's house in his car. Carol sat, silently watching the lights of the festive city of New Orleans pass by outside the window. She'd been wrong, so wrong. The whole fabric of her life had been woven of misconceptions, resentments and anger. Now it was torn to shreds, and she didn't have the strength to rebuild it.

She was unaware when Zach's strong arms lifted her sleeping form from the car and carried her upstairs. Without awakening her, he slipped her arms from the sleeves of her suit jacket and slid the skirt down over her hips, along with her panty hose. Pulling the sheet up to her shoulders, he stood for a moment, studying the smudge of mascara beneath her tear-swollen eyes, the puffiness of her face, the curve of her slight body as she curled automatically into a fetal position on the bed.

"Sweet lady, someday you'll come to me of your own free will. And only on that day will you be really free."

And he closed the bedroom door behind him and left her to sleep away the uncertainty that had staggered her usually decisive stance in life.

Carol awoke slowly, becoming aware of the unfamiliar feel of a strange bed. When she finally opened her eyes, she blinked stupidly, her eyes feeling stiff and gritty. A nagging ache in her temples was a residue of the horrible previous evening.

Just as she convinced herself to attempt untangling her mind and body, a sound behind her halted her first tentative movements.

"Awake?" Zach's low voice made her body tense.

"What if I said 'no'?" Her voice was croaky, and she swallowed to clear the cottony feeling.

"Then it goes back downstairs, and I'll drink both cups."

Surrendering to the inevitable, Carol shifted her legs and finally managed to roll to her back. As she struggled to sit up, Zach slid a tray holding a glass of orange juice and two mugs of steaming coffee onto the nightstand. Deftly he stacked pillows for her to rest on.

Self-consciously Carol combed her hair with trembling fingers.

"You look fine." Soft humor made Zach's dark eyes twinkle.

"You're a liar, but thanks."

"Try this." Zach offered the juice, and she sipped it gratefully.

There was still evidence of tears. Her eyes were stiff and puffy. It was obvious, too, that though she had slept hard, emotional exhaustion having taken its toll, she was not refreshed.

Carol finished the juice, and Zach silently handed her one of the mugs of coffee, sipping at his own as she carefully tested the strength and temperature of hers.

When Carol had taken a healthy swallow, she tried her voice again. "I don't remember arriving here last night."

"I'm not surprised. Opening your soul does strange things to the mind. Sometimes the mind shuts down until the initial shock recedes and you're better able to cope."

She glanced at him briefly, unwilling to meet his searching intuitive gaze. "Sounds like you've been there."

"I have, on occasion." He settled himself more comfortably on the bed. "You see, I took my marriage for granted. I had what I wanted—a home, an orderly life. Children would come along. I thought it was all settled. When I learned differently, it took a while to come to terms with. It was only later that I could objectively examine my feelings and realize what I'd felt was a mixture of anger that my settled world had been disturbed and injured pride. Only then could I admit the marriage was something I hadn't really worked at, the product of my doing what I thought was expected of me. Love had never really entered into it. Not for either of us."

"I've never heard you talk this way before."

A small smile moved his lips. "I discovered last night, after tucking you in, that there are a number of things we haven't discussed. I think it's time."

Carol argued with herself, unwilling to open the door to painfully revealing subjects again.

"Have you talked with John?" she asked, suspecting he had.

"No. What you discussed is between the two of you, except what you choose to tell me yourself."

Finally she could meet his intent gaze. "You're a very special man. I'm sorry I doubted you." She turned the mug carefully between her hands. "I guess I projected my own doubt and dishonesty onto you."

"That's a start," Zach encouraged her.

Carol drew a deep breath, and Zach waited. She reminded him of a very confused child. It was an image he found difficult to reconcile with the efficient and controlled woman who had very neatly engineered the near destruction of her family's business, then just as cleverly breathed life back into it.

"I learned some things last night I wish I'd known ten years ago." Zach waited as Carol laboriously formed her thoughts. "John made me face some very ugly truths about myself."

"I'm listening." Zach set his cup aside, leaving Carol's so she could have something in her hands to concentrate on.

"I thought John had things so easy. But he had pressures of a different kind to deal with from my father. To humiliate him, my father pointed out John's inadequacies. And John had to meet my father's expectations and assume responsibilities not of his choosing. Of course, there were a few things John was able to avoid. But all in all, we experienced the same kinds of anger and frustration. He just held it in better than I did."

With a long sigh, Carol scooted down in the bed and pulled the sheets up higher over her lace-edged slip. Looking at the ceiling to avoid looking at Zach, she continued her recitation. "I did John a serious injustice, thinking he and our father were aligned. I forgot how alike John and I really are. Instead of banding together with him against our father, I transferred all my anger and frustration to John." Almost to herself, she added, "I will never be able to make up for that."

When she was silent for several moments, Zach spoke. "And then what happened?"

Her head rolled toward him on the pillow. "I compounded that mistake by marrying a man who was just as demanding as my father but in other ways."

"Going by what you've told me, I'd say you weren't to blame for everything. Alex Martin wasn't exactly the faithful sort."

Her constant running of nervous fingers through her hair made the turmoil remaining inside her evident. "That's what I tell myself, but maybe..."

"Hey—" he reached for her hand and trapped it firmly between his "—it's over. It's time for new beginnings." He tugged at her hand until she obeyed and came into his welcoming arms. "All that counts now is that we both know where we made mistakes and are willing to work at a new relationship. You and John are communicating. And I hope you can now begin thinking about how you want to redecorate this house once you're Mrs. Zachary Taylor."

Doubt clouded her eyes as Carol pushed back from Zach. "John and I talked a little about the family business and the part I could play in it. Of course, it was only preliminary..."

Zach grinned widely as her words trailed off uncertainly. "Carol, I may be a man of Southern heritage, but I have no illusions about your ambition and drive. So, I take it you and John are discussing ways to combine the assets of CCC with those of DuBois?"

"Yes. A lot has to be discussed yet, but I expect to be actively involved."

"I wouldn't try to limit you in any way, sweetheart. Just leave room for me and, eventually, a couple of kids, huh?"

Doubt changed to delight as she absorbed the sincerity of his words. "Oh, Zach, you've taught me so much. I love you so."

"Ah, my lady." He gathered her to him again and pulled her down across the bed with him. "Those are the words I've been waiting to hear. How about a wedding a week from today? Sooner, if we can get a waiver on the waiting period and get things together. John can give you away, and we could have the ceremony here in the backyard. The flowers are blooming. And that paragon of virtue you call a secretary could stand up with you, order flowers, arrange for a reception. Then you'll be free to find a dress...."

Carol laughed into the curve of Zach's shoulder. "Whatever happened to that nonchalant approach to life you're so proud of? You sound very decisive, Mr. Taylor."

"Well," he said, grinning up at the face he held between his hands, "sometimes even we Cajuns can be very decisive. Any objections?"

"None at all, Mr. Zachary Taylor. None at all." And for the next little while there were no momen-

tous decisions made. There were only the quiet mur-
murs of love and the whispered words, "my Cajun
man," as they journeyed once again to that special
place known only to very special lovers.

COMING NEXT MONTH

UNLIKELY LOVER—Diana Palmer
Mari's matchmaking aunt had tricked Ward into inviting her niece to his ranch. Now it was up to them to teach Aunt Lillian a lesson. Was falling in love part of the plan?

THE CASTAWAYS—Frances Lloyd
No men allowed! was Elly's motto. Until fate decided to shipwreck her with the infamous womanizer Chester Fawkes. He was a pirate determined to possess her. ... body and soul.

FRIENDS—AND THEN SOME—Debbie Macomber
Playing piano in a hotel lounge was not Lily's idea of a promising future—it was more like a nightmare! She needed to be rescued, and Jake was just the man to do it. Now he had to convince her. ...

HEAVENLY MATCH—Sharon De Vita
Jonathan Kent was supposed to be a simple blind date, just like all the others. Instead he barged into Molly's life, turned it upside down and had the whole town talking about their heavenly match.

THE EYES OF A STRANGER—Terri McGraw
David Chandler knew nothing about running a Thoroughbred horse farm, so why was he trying? He wouldn't tell, and Dusty was beginning to wonder if he was who he said he was. ...

HERO ON HOLD—Glenda Sands
She had thought him dead—but Adam Zachery was alive and well and standing in Anna's office. Could a relationship that had been on hold for seventeen years be revived?

AVAILABLE THIS MONTH:

SWEET MOUNTAIN MAGIC
Emilie Richards

CAJUN MAN
Olivia Ferrell

BUTTERFLY AUTUMN
Carolyn Seabaugh

GOLDEN GLORY
Stella Bagwell

SHEER HONESTY
Susan Phillips

STRANGE BEDFELLOWS
Arlene James

FOUR UNIQUE SERIES
FOR EVERY WOMAN YOU ARE . . .

Silhouette Romance

Heartwarming romances that will make you
laugh and cry as they bring you all the wonder
and magic of falling in love.

6 titles
per month

Silhouette Special Edition

Expanded romances written with emotion and
heightened romantic tension to ensure
powerful stories. A rare blend of passion and
dramatic realism.

6 titles
per month

Silhouette Desire

Believable, sensuous, compelling—and
above all, romantic—these stories deliver
the promise of love, the guarantee
of satisfaction.

6 titles
per month

Silhouette Intimate Moments

Love stories that entice; longer, more
sensuous romances filled with adventure,
suspense, glamour and melodrama.

4 titles
per month

Silhouette Romances
not available in retail outlets in Canada

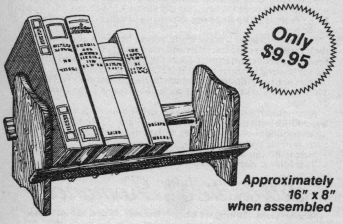

Take 4 Silhouette Romance novels
FREE

Then preview 6 brand-new Silhouette Romance® novels—delivered to your door as soon as they are published—for 15 days without obligation. When you decide to keep them, pay just $1.95 each, *with no shipping, handling or other charges of any kind!*

Each month, you'll meet lively young heroines and share in their thrilling escapades, trials and triumphs...virile men you'll find as attractive and irresistible as the heroines do...and colorful supporting characters you'll feel you've always known.

Start with 4 Silhouette Romance novels absolutely FREE. They're yours to keep without obligation, and you can cancel at any time.

As an added bonus, you'll also get the Silhouette Books Newsletter FREE with every shipment. Every issue is filled with news on upcoming books, interviews with your favorite authors, even their favorite recipes.

Simply fill out and return the coupon today!
This offer is not available in Canada.

Silhouette ❤ Romance®

Silhouette Books, 120 Brighton Rd., P.O. Box 5084, Clifton, NJ 07015-5084